Lula

Tore Fauske

Published 2009 by arima publishing

www.arimapublishing.com

ISBN 978 1 84549 389 9

© Tore Fauske 2009

Printed and bound in the United Kingdom

Typeset in Garamond 12/14

In this work of fiction, the characters, places and events are either the product of the author's imagination or they are used entirely fictitiously. Any resemblance to actual persons, living or dead, is purely coincidental.

Swirl is an imprint of arima publishing.

arima publishing

ASK House, Northgate Avenue

Bury St Edmunds, Suffolk IP32 6BB

t: (+44) 01284 700321

www.arimapublishing.com

We've been here nearly one month, Lulla. Nearly a month. That's a long time - a long time in war, with nothing but misery, killing, burning. We were sent from Texas, 123 men, and straight to the front. First in the south, then further and further north as we advanced. Three days ago we arrived at Kimpo airport - it looked bloody awful. This airport which we attacked again and again less than a week ago, doing our bloody best to obliterate, making it completely unserviceable - and now? We have to repair and defend it. Life is strange.

Life? Can you talk about, think about, life at all here? No. And yet yes. What *is* life? Nothing but a hectic, crazy whirlwind of killing - killing others, kill as many as you can before they kill you. That is life - or death. Two words, two meaningless words. Everyone wants to live - yet everyone must die. Live or die, does it matter? Not here it doesn't. But where you are, with Ian - *that* is life.

Ian? Let me forget him. Let me dream that you are mine, and mine only. It gives me strength, courage, something to live for.

"Live" - this word again. An empty word. A meaningless word. *Live - here*? - where everything dies? Peter - you didn't know Peter, a splendid chap and good friend. I saw him being shot to pieces by a MIG-15 yesterday. Perhaps he's happier now. I don't know. All I know is that I am afraid of these bloody MIG-15s. Very afraid. Scared.. They are terrifying - their 30mm canons can smash even the largest of our planes.

Our F-86s are good, but I am afraid of the Russians'. I don't like the 86s - I wish we had our old P-51s again, then, perhaps, I might not have been so frightened.

I am glad you have no idea how frightened, no: *scared stiff* I am every time we take off! I shiver and sweat - I am scared, scared of death, scared of dying, scared of being injured, shot down - just plain scared. Then we take off, looking for the enemy. I always hope we don't see a single one - and yet, at the same time, I wish we'll meet a dozen of the bastards so we can shoot them out of the sky, see them tumble like dead, mutilated ducks to the ground, throwing up smoke and dust and flames as they hit it.

That's what it is all about here, Lulla: fright, terror, killing, pieces of human bodies. Live?

You must be joking.

The first time was the worst of all. I was so scared I don't think I really knew what I was doing. It's a bit better now, not much, but a bit. But it's still there every time I climb into the cockpit, this ice-cold, paralysing fear, gnawing, eating you from inside. Until I am in the middle of it all. Then there is no time to be afraid. I don't know if the others are scared, but I think so. I know that Bobby is. He told me the other day that he is scared out of his wits every time he sits in the cockpit, parachute on, ready to take off. But he's a brave chap, Bobby. He's only 19, but he volunteered to avenge his father. He blames the Russians for his father's death in 1943: he was chief engineer on a B-17, and the Russians refused to let them land in Russia after they had been badly damaged when bombing targets in eastern parts of Germany. They never came back. Bobby is bitter with the Russians.

But he is also scared.

Look at the faces here. Look at them. Look carefully. Some are tired, some give the impression they don't care; - some are dreaming, joking - or reading. But they have one thing in common: they are willing to fight to defend and protect the life, the world, and the freedom they still have. Most of them are volunteers - young boys every one of them, young boys entitled to live like young boys. In peace. But they are here, fighting, in order that others may live. Ask them - ask them why they volunteered. Perhaps they'll give you an answer, perhaps not. They never talk about it, they never discuss it - they only do what they regard as their simple duty.

Just take Frank, on the bunk over there, staring into the ceiling. Why on Earth did he come here? Simply because he felt he had no <u>right</u> to be at home, doing nothing, when so many of his friends were being killed by the communists out here. Frank is a really nice chap, quiet, sincere, and as far from a hero-idol as you can get. But if there's one thing he cannot tolerate, it is all those staying at home, talking, and talking, but never doing anything themselves.

Or take Ashley - or Ash as he's called - sitting over there writing a letter. You certainly don't have to ask who he is writing to! He and Ann got engaged shortly before he volunteered, and you should hear and see him talk about her, Lulla! His eyes are radiant, his whole face lights up; indeed, he can hardly have any conversation at all without bringing up Ann's name. He thinks and dreams about her, night and day, I am sure. And I think he writes her a letter every day.

How often haven't I thought of writing to you, Lulla? I don't know. I did write once -but I didn't post it. Perhaps I should have done.

Of course I shouldn't! It is just you and Ian now, just the two of you. Or perhaps you are three or four ----?

You and Ian - what's that of my business? Nothing! Nothing whatever! I know. But I do envy Ian, Lulla, good God how I envy him! But let me forget Ian - let me think about you as being mine. Think of you! I hardly do anything else! You are in my thoughts wherever I am, whatever I am doing, it is ..

Do I remember the day I met you? What a question! - Is life other than a sequence of fortuitous events? Does it serve any purpose at all to plan, think, contemplate - when all life does is to give you a kick up the arse and send you in whichever direction it feels like sending you at that particular time? Had I been only half a minute earlier, or later, I would never have known you existed. **Half a minute! 30 seconds!** That's all it took fate to push me your way.

If I hadn't happen to walk round the corner of the office

building where you worked as you struggled to lock the door behind you, arms full of books, I wouldn't have been here. A large, heavy, brown wooden door, with two small panes of glass near the top and a huge, wrought iron door handle. You looked so totally, charmingly helpless, trying to pull the door to behind you, without dropping any of the books. And if the top one hadn't slid slowly and gently off the pile, hitting the pavement with a soft thud, it is more than likely that I would have walked by without saying a word, for all I could see you were desperately struggling to hold on to the door AND to the stack of books. Did you look like a girl in utter despair!

"I'll pick it up," I said. Or something like that, anyway. It was a small book in a soft cover, the sort you keep day-to-day accounts in, and I took some of the other books off you, to let you lock the door.

"Thanks!" you said. And smiled. And those dimples! And the blonde hair, <u>nearly</u> reaching you shoulders, dancing freely and happily whenever you moved your head.

And you ask if I remember?

You looked utterly helpless and tiny. Your eyes were radiantly alive and smiling - and your *smile* and your *voice!* The world and I stopped for a moment - I did not know what to say, what to do - did I just stand there with open mouth, looking gormless? I think I did.

"Thanks! You appeared just at the right moment!"

All I could do was listening to your voice - spellbound by your smile.

You had a light mac on, and little white boots. Do I remember it, Lulla!

I asked, no, I mumbled and stuttered something about "Do you always carry arms full of books?" and you laughed and said that no, you didn't, but your boss had asked if you would be kind enough to check the accounts before the week-end - and said you might take them home if you would rather do that than sit late in the office.

"That's why," you said, and those dimples appeared again. "I am just walking to the taxi rank to get a taxi home."

Of course I offered to carry the books to the taxi rank for you - for all it was only a two minutes' walk. All whilst my thoughts were spinning as I tried to keep some sort of sane and sensible conversation going.

I remember that an elderly couple was waiting at the rank, and we stopped behind them.

"What about cinema tomorrow?" I heard a voice say. "You are not sitting checking the books night and day, are you?" the voice carried on, and I wondered who it was talking.

You hesitated.

"There's a Danny Kaye film on that's supposed to be very funny" said the voice, which I gradually began to recognise as my own. The voice omitted to say that I had seen it only the evening before. "What about it?"

A taxi arrived, and the couple in front got in. The next taxi would be yours.

You hesitated. "Well, no - I don't know --. I don't know

you --."

That's when the taxi pulled up. It was one of the brand new Studebakers, looking the same from the front as from the back - you remember, all the jokes about them, such as: "The trouble with these models is that you don't know whether it has just run over you - or is just about to do so!"

"Make it a date!" I said as you got into the taxi. "I'll be outside your office door at 6.30pm - yes?"

"I don't know," you said through the half open window as the taxi moved away. But your eyes said "yes" - didn't they?

Your eyes said "Yes", Lulla!

I didn't know about Ian, then.

I was outside your office door long before 6.30 pm the next day. It was raining, and I was sheltering in the little porch, taking a few steps out onto the pavement every minute or so, afraid that if you DID come - IF you came - you might not see me.

How time dragged! How I waited and waited - and feared you might not turn up. I had already made my mind up that if you didn't come, I would be outside your office door every afternoon until I saw you again.

It was nearly a quarter to seven when you came running - or run as best you could with the umbrella up. When I spotted the white boots my heart skipped a beat or two, - no, it did more than that: it jumped wildly around before finally settling back into its normal pace and place.

It took some time.

It was the bus, you said - it pulled away just as you arrived at the bus stop, so you had to wait for the next one.

So what the heck! You had arrived - you were here, with me.

We talked about all and nothing – I had difficulties thinking straight, and I am sure I stuttered and waffled a lot; you must have thought I was a bit of a twit.

We DID see the Danny Kaye-film, didn't we? I'm far from sure - all I heard and noticed and still remember was your contagious, happy laughter.

It was still raining when we came out, and you put the umbrella up. When I took it to shelter us both you put your arm under mine as if we had been together for a long, long time; looked at me - and smiled.

Could you feel the tingling, bubbling sensation of excitement and happiness that raced through me? I am sure everyone around us could see and sense my feelings - feelings so strong, so vibrant and intense that I don't think I really understood it myself.

You had to catch the first bus home, you said. I wanted to see you home, but you said No. You had promised your mother you would come straight home afterwards.

"What about tomorrow? Do I see you tomorrow?" I am sure there was a touch of anxiety - even desperation in my voice. A wave of fear and doubt swelled up inside me.

"Tomorrow?" I said again.

"Perhaps," you said. "Give me a ring in the office."

But I was telling you about Ash. He volunteered as well. He was young and healthy - he had no choice but to follow his conscience and do his duty. Thousands of his countrymen were fighting and dying for freedom and democracy, and it would be unfair to stay at home and pretend the world was full of peace. We are in eternal debt to those who die for us - a debt which can only be repaid by completing the task they began. To fail, to avoid doing anything, is to betray them. Or even worse: it helps the enemy. We must not fail, we cannot live peacefully as long as communism or any other -ism is threatening the whole world, freedom and personal choice. That's why Ash volunteered. He would rather, much rather, be at home with Ann; set up a home, start a family and live in peace and harmony. How he is longing for this war to finish! This unnecessary, terrible butchering started by the human race, probably the only living creature which kills simply for the sake of killing - and not to fill the stomach. The most intelligent of all intelligent beings, applying their high intelligence to think up more effective and more horrendous methods of exterminating each other. For each day Ash spent at home, his conscious troubled him more and more. In the end he did what he felt he had to do. It was hard, very hard, to say goodbye to Ann, but she agreed with him: he had no moral right to stay at home.

She must be quite a girl, Ann!

He's not the only one. Most of them volunteered because they regarded it as their simple duty to do so. They had no choice. Young boys, staring death in the eyes every day, strengthened in the knowledge that they are just doing the job they have to do.

Perhaps with two exceptions: Bill Croony and Sam Carter. They are here for the one and only reason that they like excitement. They love danger and revel in high odds stacked against them. They're just like kids every time they are fighting superior forces - with every possibility of being pulverized. Two rebels who couldn't care less about orders and authority. I envy them - of course I do! - imagine to be like them; courageous, daring, cheerful and joking whatever the situation. They stick together like twins, in the air and on the ground.

Sam always calls Bill "Lofty": he is a giant, too tall and big for a fighter pilot, really. They didn't want to take him at first, the Colonel said he would need his own hangar. But after he had climbed into the cockpit of a Corsair, and showed them what he could do, they took him. On the spot.

I don't think they've regretted it.

Sam is as small and slim as Bill is big and strong. But as tough as they come. And always playing practical jokes on everybody.

It's surprising nobody has nicknamed them "Laurel and

Hardy".

God, am I afraid, Lulla! I am trembling all over, I can hardly move my hands. But you must - you MUST! Throttle forward, slowly, slowly --! Listen to the whine of the engine, a whistling-like sound. Stop that bloody shaking! It's only a recce-trip!

There - Bobby is taxiing out. Poor Bobby, he's just as scared as I am. Now -- now, it's my turn! Easy - take it easy - calm down! That heart! It's beating away like a steam-hammer.

Turn, now - yes, that's it. Then throttle. Remember the compressor - that's it. Everything is OK. These blasted 86s - I don't like them - it's no good. Why can't we have 51s?

Take her nicely up now. That's it. Undercarriage in? Yes. Fine!

Where are the others? There - there they are! Fall into place now, behind Frank - keep your station.

It looks as if we are standing still up here. But look down - look down, Lulla! They go much too fast, these flying stoves, much too fast!

I prefer a Spit or a 51.

All six are in position. Frank is in front of me, George behind me. On my right wing I have Bill, Sam, and Bobby. Only six of us today - just a quick recce.

The dots down there are our tanks. They are close to the front now. Poor devils on the ground. We have a chance, at least. But they? Not a chance in hell.

What is it? Frank must have spotted something, I think.

"Hello Barnet Blue! Attack in open formation, column at 2 o'clock. Only two sweeps. Come on!"

Column? 2 o'clock? Oh - yes, I can see them! Looks like lorries. Here we go! Dive -slight rudder. Is the turn indicator correct? Yes - all is OK.

I am not scared or trembling any more, can you see, Lulla? This is different - now it's the poor bastards down there who are scared - scared to be shot to pieces. Look how fast they're approaching! Lorries - lorries full of people. Soldiers. Human beings. "Shoot - shoot to kill! Kill them!" That's an order. And orders must be obeyed. It's them or us.

Either - or. It's never "both - and". Always either - or. They have guns, can you see the tracers streaming up towards us, Lulla? But don't worry, Lulla, these mobile, little guns aren't all that frightening. The big ones are a different matter.

Do you remember the photograph you gave me? I have it in front of me in the cockpit, between all the instruments. Allowed? Bloody hell - no! It's strictly forbidden - I would have been severely disciplined if they found out. But they won't, they'll never know about it. Here it's just you and me. I always take it down before we land. But I always carry it with me. Always.

Now! First the guns, then the rockets. There --! That's

what I call bullseye! Two of the lorries are engulfed in flames already - with soldiers jumping off all the others, running for cover. Some manage - others don't. One--two--three - three of my rockets sent on their deadly way. I can't see if they hit, have to turn away. Stick hard towards you - rudder. Watch the trim! Not too much!

So - that's it. Fine. Neat turn now. There's Bobby. He's smiling now, I am sure. He is always smiling when he fires.

Stick forward - and slight rudder again - straight down. We have done a good job. Nearly all of the lorries burning, only a few are still moving. After them - get them! Destroy them - kill! Kill! The road is covered in bodies, dead, wounded. But remember: it's them or us. Either - or! Don't forget that!

There are the lorries - let go rockets! All I can see is a slight streak of what looks like smoke as they hurtle towards the targets, bringing death and destruction. Poor sods!

Up again, find your place in the formation - everyone here?

Yes, six. Now, let's see what we have done.

This is what the telegrams describe as "a successful attack". Successful to destroy great values, kill and mutilate human beings, humans like us, youngsters like us.

"Successful".

We can't see the lorries any more - just the smoke billowing up, far away. They're fast, these 86s. Too bloody fast - you don't get time to think. I don't like this speed, more than

400mph is no fun. And these manage something like 600mph - much too fast. And you can't reduce the speed too much; if you do, you stall. The wings are too short, small and at the wrong angle. Mitchell was the man - he knew how to design aeroplanes!

Frank's turning - we're heading home again.

Did I say "home"? A misnoma if ever there was one. Back to base, back to the mess, back to debriefing, reports - and new raids. There was some talk about an early morning raid tomorrow, two squadrons, some major attack on two heights. *That's* what we're going "home" to.

And we're nearly there already --. Much to bloody fast, this.

I am sure I have said it before, so what? Does it matter? Here, nothing matters. Only kill, kill, kill --. Or be killed. It's the "either - or". This war, ANY war, numbs your feelings and senses, degrades you from a human being to a machine, a robot, blindly executing orders, Executing - a good word here, don't you think? But Bobby, only 19 - he's too young for this.

Frank is down. Stick forward, throttle back - keep an eye on the speedo. These damned things stall where a good old Spit would keep on gliding. Undercarriage down - all OK? Green light. So, gently down, fuel off, - remember the compressor! Roll a little before applying the brakes. Not too hard! Instruments - OK? Yes, all in order.

Well, out you get!

Wow! I nearly forget your picture, Lulla! Good thing I

spotted it as I was about to climb out!

"Successful," said the Officer. What did I say? And no doubt it was: 70% of the lorries totally destroyed, and how many soldiers killed? Your guess is as good as mine, but a hell of a lot of young men, like us, killed and maimed. How more successful can you be?

Now it's time to get some food and sleep - we're off tomorrow morning again, 24 of us, 86s that is. Some heights, as we heard mentioned.

"We have to do a thorough job," said the briefing officer, "making it as easy as we can for our boys when they storm the heights. Understood?"

Understood all right. We'll make a thorough job, be sure.

***

I telephoned you the next day - I had to fight against an all-consuming desire to ring you first thing in the morning. Somehow I managed to wait until after lunch. How?

I don't know.

Your voice was enough to send my heart racing again. I vaguely remember I mumbled something about "It was a nice evening last night" - and "Do I see you again tonight?", and very clearly the feeling of darkest despair when you said you couldn't -you were going out with a girlfriend.

"But what about the next day?" I asked. The next day - some far-away time into the distant future! I wanted to see you today - NOW! Perhaps you could detect the fear in my voice - fear that I would never see you again?

You hesitated - didn't know. Perhaps --. "Ring me tomorrow," you said.

Anguish - is that the word? In one short moment I had plunged from the highest hopes and expectations to the deepest pit full of total darkness and emptiness. And all because you did not say "Yes" straight away. If you had known how I suffered that day, Lulla! All I wanted was to see you again, talk to you, be with you, listen to you, hear your happy laughter - feel you near me.

It was a year until the next day.

It wasn't funny.

Next day - do you know I lifted the receiver three times to ring you - only to replace it. I was terrified, absolutely terrified, that you would say "no" once more. That you would make some pretext or the other for not being able to see me. I didn't have the courage to ring you - and hear the verdict.

Not until just before I thought you were going home.

"When you hadn't telephoned by 4pm," you said, "I thought you didn't want to ring me."

Didn't want to ring you! Not ring you? Having suffered every minute of the day, wanting, desperately, to ring you, but not daring to?

The first I noticed when you got off the bus, was your hair. It was shorter. And it made you look even more gorgeous, sexier.

I think I ran towards you the moment you got off. Or perhaps I didn't. Perhaps I walked. But I wanted to run - run and leap and hug you and lift you and swirl you round and hold you and kiss you, never to let you go.

You smiled, put your arm under mine and pushed me straight up and into the seventh heaven.

We wandered about a bit, looking in shop windows, talking about all and everything. Then we walked into the park, do you remember? Who suggested it, or who was leading whom, I have no idea - all I could register was that you were next to me, talking to me, smiling at me, what else could I care about, what else would I notice? Nothing else mattered.

We stopped on the little bridge across the small lake, remember? Looking down into the water reflecting the light from the lamp.

Did I want to kiss you! Tell you that I loved you, needed you - you, and nobody else. If only you knew. Perhaps you did - I don't think I am a good actor; I found it difficult not to show you what I felt.

But I was also afraid. Afraid that I might frighten you away - afraid that you might think I was only after a pleasant evening or two - and then forget you.

Forget you!

That's why I was so clumsy and awkwardly helpless, trying to keep a lid on the stormy and boiling feelings inside me. At the same time as I was afraid that you might think I was a stupid, bumbling fool; doing nothing but talk nonsense and being tongue-tied as soon as I came anywhere near a girl.

How long we were in the park? I have no idea. All I remember is the intense feeling of elation and happiness - and the fear that unless I "behaved", I might not see you again. Ever.

Either - or.

Either I behaved - or I'd never see you again.

We stopped at the big tree, the one the other side of the bridge. That's when I nearly - NEARLY! - lost my senses.

And you noticed!

We ran empty for words; just stood there. I was quite certain that you expected me, *wanted* me, to kiss you – am I not right, Lulla?! I held one arm round you, you rested your head on my shoulder.

Could you hear my heart thumping away? Of course you could! People at the other end of the park could hear it! All the world could hear it!

That's when the fear, that nagging, consuming fear, returned. I knew you wanted me to kiss you - I knew what you were thinking, and still: that fear was a barrier. The fear that I might never see you again. And the fear that you might feel convinced that I was a useless bundle of nerves. A bumbling idiot.

God - did I suffer, Lulla!

I wanted to see you home, but you said no. Again.

And that was enough to scare me, really scare me, once more! I *knew* it! I should have kissed you there in the park - shown you that I loved you, needed you - told you that I loved you and needed you.

Instead, I just stood there like a gormless, fumbling fool.

When you got on the bus that evening, my whole life disappeared with you.

It was awful. Bloody awful.

I think I cried.

We were up early today. The attack is to take place at 07.53. It's 07.28 now. Not 07.25 or 07.27. It's very strict here. Very accurate. Not like life where you are - 07.25 or 07.27 - does it matter?

Take-off is in 8 minutes. 12 of us. On my immediate left is Frank, on my right is Ash. Jimmy is leading today, good chap, Jimmy - veteran from '45. He prefers the 51 as well - although his favourite is the P-38. But not here, he says - they're too slow.

I don't think I agree --.

These are too fast. Much too fast. They don't give you time to think. To react. 600 is far too fast--.

Of course I am afraid. I am always afraid. Scared. Nothing in particular - just scared. Perhaps I'm afraid of the MIG-15s, perhaps I'm afraid of death. But why? Can anything be worse than this living hell? I doubt it.

But I don't want to die! I want to live - LIVE! Even the most wretched clings to life, clutches at straws in desperate despair. It is called "Hope"!

It's 07.32. The first one is starting. One after the other, better get my act together. This is when I am most afraid, Lulla - fear is gripping me, tearing at my inside, making me shake and tremble so it is difficult to do what I have to do. These seconds just before take-off --!

Pull yourself together!

Jimmy is off, with Ralph just behind. Frank is moving out.

Concentrate! Don't look at the picture! For Pete's sake - concentrate! Move off, turn a bit - that's it. Throttle - more throttle - DON'T LOOK AT THE PICTURE! Frank is airborne, by the tower. I'll take her a bit further - only a few metres. Now - stick towards you - steady, evenly. OK - you're up. Undercarriage up - more throttle, and more height. Listen to that sound, that whining, roaring sound, Lulla!

Everyone up? Yes - there's George - the last one. Fall in - then northwards.

I am Barnet Blue 3. Jimmy is Red 1, behind him is Bobby. Ralph is No 3, and George No. 4. Frank is Yellow 1, his No 2 is a new chap, Bud. He came in after Peter. Ash is No 3, and Ernie McKinley is No 4. He's a tough Scot.

It's now 07.43. We should meet the other twelve in 2 minutes. 2 minutes EXACTLY. We're still over our area, see some of the chaps below waving to us? A last farewell? Perhaps it is - perhaps it isn't. I don't now. Nobody knows anything here. We just think, guess, hope. Hope? *Here?* You must be joking!

There are some dots. MIGs? One, two, three, four -- twelve. Must be ours. But you never know - you just hope. That word "hope" again!

Bloody speed!

Yes, they're 86s - falling in behind us. So we're in first. Good - they have had more time to get their aim right when the second wave comes in! So Jimmy is leading the lot.

Good chap Jimmy.

We're nearly there, Lulla. Are you scared? I am. Do you think they have 88s? Hope not. Have you ever dived straight at the devils with 88 mm rushing towards you? Of course you haven't! And keep praying that you never will! Just one single hit - and you are blown into fragments and scattered like bloody bits round the countryside. Literally. Think about it - bloody bits! Literally.

Can you see how I perspire? Sweating - and shivering?

It's 07.52.40. There! The heights. Two cosy looking hills, the sort of hills you would be taking a Sunday walk on. Hills full of grazing sheep.

But not here. Here they are hills full of ugly scars caused by our artillery. We have hammered these hills mercilessly most of the night.

But don't let that fool you! There's plenty of the bastards left down there, just waiting, - ready to receive us, aiming their guns at us. Just wait and see!

There - Jimmy breaks off, diving straight down. I can see his tracers. And there - what did I say, Lulla? They're opening up with all they've got!

There goes Frank - and Bud - and Bobby.

Hell has broken loose.

Hell is the right word. If only you had time to think! But you mustn't think. Just act. Act and react, quickly, fast, automatically.

Suddenly the world is upside-down. Aeroplanes, flames,

smoke, fire, more planes - tracers from the ground and up - and from the planes and down. What's up and what's down in this hectic, lunatic dance?

Down - fire! Fire! As low as you can, fill the burnt, blackened remains of the forest below you with lead - then up again - joystick hard back - throttle - QUICK! STEEP! And down again. Up - down - up. Planes everywhere, in every direction. It's a sheer wonder we don't collide in this crazy, boiling mess.

You can't see anything down there - just tracers meeting you, streaming up from that blackened forest in slow motion. So what the hell! Just keep pumping bullets down - fill the whole bloody landscape with them! Our rockets are doing a grand job - churning up the soil, flinging stones and earth - and pieces of people - towards us in a grim greeting.

I am calm now, Lulla. Not scared any more. Even though they do have some 88s. But we'll give them many times 88s! Many times!

Time and place don't exist any more - time and place have been obliterated. The only things which exist here are smoke, fire, death, and destruction. And machines with cold, cynical robot-like murderers.

WOW! That was close!

It's too fast, this.

Oi - did you see that, Lulla? We must have hit an

ammunition dump - have you ever SEEN such fireworks? I could feel the blast up here - what in hell is it like down there?

LOOK! Someone is waving a white flag! Good - now our chaps can take over - the first ones are already on their way up the slope. OK, Jimmy, well done! Let's return to base.

Are we all here? I can't see the other twel --, yes, there they are.

But what's that? Some small dots, growing rapidly. Do you think, - YES - it is! MIGs! One, two, three --- seventeen, eighteen -- I make it more than thirty! More than thirty MIG-15s!

Dear God - don't let one of their 30mm hit me!

There's Jimmy: "Hello, Barnet Red leader calling! MIG-15s in from 11 o'clock. Battle formation. Barnet Blue and Yellow - open up, the flank. Good luck!"

Good luck! You need more than bloody good luck against thirty MIG-15s!

We are taking the right flank. If only my heart would not pump away like that! Take it easy! We're peeling off - 4 of us. I bet Bill and Sam are enjoying this! If only I had their courage and nerves. They're chatting to each other - picking out their targets. You should think they were out shooting ducks!

"Hello Blue 4, Blue 3 calling. Keep behind me and cover my back. Look out for decoys, don't chase anyone too far - OK?"

"Roger."

There they are. Bloody hell what speed! Everything OK? Oil pressure? Fuel? Ammunition - yes, still over half left. Cockpit pressure correct? Reflector aimer?

Ready. THERE! I have got one in my sight. Ra-ta-ta-ta-. And we're miles past each other.

Rudder - hard rudder - TURN! CLIMB! FAST! FAST! Sam's got one on his tail. Rudder! MORE! THERE - give it to him!

Did you see that, Lulla? Did you see how he exploded, blown to pieces? Scattered all over the heavens? More like that!

Phooui! That was only just! I thought I touched him! It was --. Look, Bill is chasing one. He's enjoying this, Bill.

LOOK OUT! That one, coming out of the sun! Stick hard forward, throttle, rudder, stick towards you again - hard! It's a wonder the plane isn't disintegrating. Can't understand how it can take it - the speedo is showing 665 mph! SIX HUNDRED and SIXTY-FIVE, Lulla! Perhaps they're not all that bad after all, these kites? But nearly 700 is too much.

There he is again! Give him a short burst - that's all he needs. THERE! He's hit, Lulla, he's hit! He's jumping! He's jumping, Lulla! That's TWO MIGs in one day - TWO of them! Now I am not afraid any longer! Just let them come, 30 mm and all! Just come, bloody devils, just come! *Two* MIGs – *yippee*!! That's four all told. Perhaps a 51 wouldn't.

"Look out, Frank!! LOOK OUT - you have one on your tail - FRANK!!"

He can't hear me. How could he? But the radio - the RADIO! But where is Bud? There - behind Frank. No - he isn't, he *should* have been there - but he isn't. Bud -BUD!

I can't see him. But I MUST see what's happening to Frank. I must! FRANK - look out!

But can anyone see and follow anything at all in this melé? Is any human being able to react and register anything at all in this crazy, speedy world where Life and Death stand hand in hand, grinning at you? Friend or foe - how the bloody hell can anyone tell who --.

THAT was close! I think he hit the cockpit. And nearly the picture of you, Lulla. But only nearly. If THAT is hit, I am hit as well. You and me. Together.

Like it should have been - but isn't.

Who the hell was that who shot past, trailing smoke? A murder machine having received a fatal blow, shooting like a helpless meteorite towards the earth, down there. Or is it up there? Up - down - who the hell can tell what is where in this wild dance with Death? Friend or foe - it all blurs into one. But it mustn't. You *must not* make a mistake. Hesitate a fraction of a second, and you'll never --.

There they are again. It's not Frank who's got one on his

tail - it's Ash! It's the same MIG, I am sure, - a skilful pilot. Perhaps he was trained by the Americans during the War. Ash has seen him - he's twisting and turning and rolling, but the bastard is following his every move. He's no beginner.

"I'll help you, Ash, I'll help you!"

Where's Ernie? I can't see him - haven't time to look for him.

Did I complain about too much speed? Even with the throttle pressed full forward it's not fast enough. Please God, more speed - FASTER!

THERE! I've got him. Can you feel the faint vibrations, Lulla - the guns beating the rhythm. The rhythm of Death. It is --.

NO! It can't be. IT CAN'T BE!"
"Ash, Ash - can you hear me - ASH!?"

Ann, poor Ann!

The bloody bastard! He got Ash, but I'll avenge you, Ash - I'll avenge you a thousand times over! I'll get him - be sure! Smash his skull in, grind him into minute bits and scatter him like dusty powder all over his fellow bastards down there! I have got him - right in my sights, like he had you, Ash. I've got him! HE HASN'T SEEN ME, ASH!

Now it is his turn - do you hear me, Ash - IT'S HIS

TURN! He stuck to you for too long and forgot to look up - look round. Behind.

Forget where you are for just a moment - no, a *fraction* of a moment, and it's your turn.

And now it is his, Ash, - it's his!

Ra-ta-ta-ta-ta-ta .. That's the longest series I have ever sent on its way, Ash. But this one is from you. From you and Ann. Look how his wings and body are being torn apart. To bits. Fragments peeling off, shooting past me. He's rolling over - there's his belly! One more round --. That's it. That's enough. Follow him - follow him down - to hell with rules and regulations and orders not to follow too far - follow him - follow him! Don't let him go for a moment - don't let him fool you!

I need not bother any more. He's dropping out of the sky like a burning torch. A burning torch - can you see, Ash? And he hasn't jumped - he hasn't jumped!

There! That was quite some impact!

Now - fast up again!

Suddenly it is all over. Where, only a few seconds ago, the world and heavens seemed to consist of nothing but planes spitting fire, twisting and turning in some form of dance macabre - there's suddenly nothing. Or very little. Gone are the MIGs - it's just us, a handful, left.

It's eerie.

Poor Ann, Lulla! They were engaged and due to marry as soon as he came home again. Look at the tears rolling slowly down Ann's face, Lulla - can you see? She should have seen Ash - I am sure he got one or two of them before they got him.

But that's not much help to her, is it?

It was two days before I saw you again. Two long, very long, days. Did I suffer! I was dazed, confused, impatient. All my thoughts were about you, and nothing else. Just you. When, the day after that evening in the park, you said you could not come to the cinema or see me at all that evening, the world collapsed round me. It was terrible. I felt awful. I think I cried. I'm not sure - the rest of that day has been deleted from my brain like a bad, nasty dream.

Never had I suffered like that before, believe me.

I seemed to remember I telephoned you several times over many days before you said yes, you could see me that evening. Was it really a mere TWO days?

And I remember the film we saw - Walt Disney's "Make mine music". Do you remember that? That is, I remember the title - not so much the film itself. All I registered, and all that is engraved on my mind, was that you were sitting next to me. What else mattered?

It was also the first time I saw you home.

Do you remember, Lulla? When we came out again after the film you wanted to catch the first bus home. More than enough to send me down into the deepest despair again. Not that I had any definite plans - all I wanted to do was to be with you. Near you. Next to you. WHERE did not matter, as long as you were there.

So when you said you wanted to go straight home --!

We walked to the bus stop not far from the cinema, but since there were a lot of people waiting I suggested we might as well walk to the next stop - or perhaps even the one after that.

You said yes, probably without realising that I would have suggested anything under the sun if only it meant I could be with you. Walk next to you. Hold your hand. Play for time. Our time.

We walked along, holding hands, and I enjoyed, *lived*, every step, every second.

The first bus passed us when we were half way between two stops. I hoped you wouldn't notice that it was your bus, fearing that you would not walk a single step further than to the next stop, and wait there. And bring my elated happiness to a sudden end.

But you did. Of course.

"Let's go a bit further," you said. "It was full."

If anyone had asked me to WALK from the cinema to where you lived, I would normally have given them short shift. See to which extent you had already then changed my way of thinking, my attitudes - all of me? We walked and walked, chatted and laughed, holding hands. I was intoxicated with happiness, I walked without moving my legs. I was floating on air. Time did not exist. Until you said: "Well, here we are. I am home."

Your mother was at home, but because it was late you didn't want me to come up. We said goodnight in the porch.

You didn't REALLY expect me to suppress my feelings

any longer, did you? It was like a dam bursting - an avalanche - an explosion, all in one.

You must admit you did not resist all that much when I kissed you. Long, deep, and intensely. And what I had not dared to hope, even think about, happened! Yes, Lulla, it did!

It was not only MY dam bursting - it was yours as well! You flung your arms round my neck and pulled me down, closer to you - never had I put so many feelings into a kiss. Never.

And you, Lulla?

Your whole body shook. Vibrated. Trembled. You pressed against me, making my blood racing burning hot through my veins, - you dug your nails into my neck and pressed yourself against me as if you wanted to make us into one.

How long we stood like that? Don't ask me - I haven't the remotest idea. How could you expect me to keep track of time! Two minutes? An eternity?

My whole body was burning - burning for you.

I remember that one of my hands wandered down your back and round to one of the buttons on your coat. It wasn't easy, the way we were pressed together. But you eased your body slightly sideways, do you remember? so that I could unbutton the coat. And when my hand found one of your breasts and I felt the nipple through the jumper, you did not object, did you, Lulla?

"I love you, Lulla - I love you!" I managed to gasp when

we had to draw breath after that very long and very hot kiss. "I love you!"

Suddenly you pushed me away. Gently, nearly reluctantly.

"No, please," you whispered. "No - don't - PLEASE! Let me go - mother is waiting. I MUST go - please!" You had as much difficulties with your breathing as I had with mine - don't deny it! You HAD, Lulla! We were both very close to breaking point. Perhaps I was even past it. I don't know. How can I? It was all too much.

"But, but--." What could I say. What SHOULD I say?

"Will you ring me tomorrow?" you asked as you half stumbled, half ran, up the steps to the door.

Before I could gather my thoughts to answer you, if an answer was needed, I heard a door shut.

Your door.

It was a long way home.

Ash was the only one from our squadron who got killed. The other squadron also lost one man. But the Reds lost nine aircraft confirmed, two probably downed, and four damaged. Of those nine, I bagged three - what happened? THREE in ONE fight! Do you know, that's a record! It's only Lofty who's managed the same - Sam's record in one go is two. So far.

I'm Yellow leader next time. - THREE MiGs; that's six all told! I'm sure it is the picture of you doing it, Lulla. Three MiG-15s!

It is empty after Ash. It is always the same - those not coming back leave an empty space, physically and mentally. We all try to pretend nothing has happened, carry on as before, tell the same jokes; if we didn't, we would go mad. But it's all a façade. Role-play.

But it is different with Ash. He was the best of us all, by far. Everyone liked him. I am sure we're all thinking about exactly the same: Ann. Nobody said anything in the mess - just ate a little, picked a bit in the food, and left.

We stretched out on our bunks afterwards, lost - didn't really know what to do. That's when Ralph suddenly mumbled, just audible, but straight from the soul of us all:

"Poor Ann."

Bobby dried away a tear. Nobody seemed to notice. I think we all had enough to control that lump in the throat.

But surely we should be *used* to this by now! Don't we experience murder, killing, mutilation, and nothing but despair and sufferings every single day? Don't we kill to the best - very best - of our ability? Are we different from the enemy?

Yes, we are! WE are defending democracy and freedom - THEY are trying to destroy democracy and freedom. That's the difference. And may we never forget that, Lulla -never.

But death and suffering take on a different dimension the moment you are personally affected. In most cases it is a question of mere statistics, numbers, faceless characters having lived somewhere you don't know about or care to know about, more often than not without even a line in a newspaper, simply lumped together with umpteen other unknowns.

But not with Ash. A young life taken away. A young human being is no more. A friend - suddenly torn away by this brutal war. No doctor, no scientist can bring him or anyone else back. It's finished - over and out.

Suddenly death itself has penetrated under the mask of coldness and carelessness you have put on - HAVE to put on to survive. You discover, suddenly and perhaps reluctantly, that you are a human being. You breathe, you feel, you think.

That's when it all seems pointless and senseless and scares you.

But be sure: we'll avenge you, Ash! We'll avenge you! As if that will do any good, as if that will bring you back! Has it ever done any good? Has it ever changed the world and made it better?

No. Never.

But you were the one of us who had the most to live for, to look forward to. You and Ann. If only for her sake, Ash - we'll avenge you, be sure! Before we have finished we'll have got our revenge, be sure! And here will be new ones to avenge, every day. More and more. Plenty more.

It is war.

Last evening, in the tent which passes for "The Mess" here, Ralph – you don't know him, of course - suddenly said: "Hands up all those who hate the North Koreans?" I think all of us did. "Why?" he asked – and we asked him what he meant.

"*Why* do you hate them? Have you ever met one, face to face; spoken to someone from North Korea, had a drink with one? Do you *know* any North-Korean?"

We thought he had turned crazy.

I am beginning to think he hadn't – it's the rest of us, the rest of the world, who has.

"If our leaders – our politicians – hadn't told us that these are the bad guys – would we know? *They* are the ones who want to go to war – do we want to? Do you? You? You?" - he pointed at each of us.

"Of course you don't!" he carried on as the rest of us sat in silence. "Wouldn't you much, much rather be at home – in the office, on your farm – at college – wherever – than doing your best to kill people you don't know, have never seen and you know little or nothing about? What we are really doing is doing the dirty work for the politicians. Why don't they do it themselves?"

Perhaps wars should be fought by politicians. People never start wars, do they? When was the last time people – or to use the politicians' favourite term: "The People" marched as one on a national assembly, demanding that the country went to war? You tell me! It is always the politicians, our leaders, who beat the drums and stir up feelings. So why don't they do the fighting themselves and leave the rest of us out of it?

It's two days since Ash was shot down - two long days. We haven't done much; flown a few sorties, repaired bits and pieces - and relaxed. As best we can.

And now we're waiting for the start signal; assisting some B-29s in trouble a bit further north.

They're dangerous, these B-29s. Quite a bite, they have, I'll tell you!

Harry is onboard one of them.

Of course, you don't know Harry, do you? We were together at the first base we had. A really nice chap. He's a gunner on one of the 29s, wanted to be a pilot, but didn't quite make it for some reason or the other. But he's a bloody good gunner. He must be, since he's only known as "Killer". "Killer" - it says everything about what we are here for, what we are doing. To kill. As many, much, and often as we can. Kill. It's an order. Full stop.

There's the signal - scramble! Run like mad to the plane, climb in - fast! Twelve of us, Jimmy leading again. It's his last trip; he's due to go home on extended leave. Frank will take over as leader, and I'll move up as Barnet Blue Leader. Today I'm "Yellow". Frank is "Blue".

That fear again! Won't it ever stop? Won't I ever get used to this? No, never. Not until there's no more to be afraid of. Nothing.

There - Sam's off. It's my turn. Movements I could do in my sleep, I think, and just as well. No time to *think*.

What the hell are you trembling for? What are you afraid

of? All you have to do is scare off some bloody MIGs - remember: you've got SIX already! THEY are the ones who should be afraid - not YOU!

Perhaps they are. Perhaps the bastards flying the MIGs are just as scared as I am. If they have human feelings at all. I don't know.

But they are dangerous, these MIGs! A 30mm can tear you to bits, remember!

I wonder if the 29s have got some of the MIGs? I am sure they have, they're certainly able to give as good as they get. Even without a 30mm. And they have done away with two trains full of troops and some bridges. Two trains. Full of soldiers. That's a hell of a lot of soldiers, Lulla! A hell of a lot of soldiers - humans - blasted to smithereens, tiny pieces. Just like Ash and Peter. Ash and Peter! We'll avenge you, both of you - be bloody sure! We'll pay them back!

There they are. I can't see exactly how many - about 30, I think. Beautiful planes. Slim, streamlined - superb. First class killing machines.

They're certainly in trouble: the MIGs are swarming round them like bees. And there - one of the 29s is rolling gently over, seems to hesitate - and then heading straight down. Haven't time to see if there are any parachutes - lets' get the MIGs!

I am leading one section - and look, Lulla, LOOK! The

MIGs are breaking off the attacks, turning and heading for home! LOOK! They're fleeing - for all they are superior in numbers! They're afraid, Lulla, they're afraid! After them, down, down, faster! Full throttle - FULL THROTTLE - faster - faster!

What the hell is Jimmy doing? Does he think ---?

THERE he is - right in my sights! It's a marvellous feeling to swoop like that on the enemy, from behind and above, straight out of the sun. He's mine, helpless as a chicken - there! He has spotted me, twisting, but too late. See how my bullets are ripping along his fuselage and across the cockpit?

Blast! He disappeared! Where is he?

I am too low, GET UP - GET UP AGAIN! See anything? Where - what?

I can't --, YES! There's Bill. I'm sure it is Bill, only he --. So Sam can't be far away - no, there he is! And there's Jimmy again, sticking like he's glued to a red devil.

Down again - that one, on the wing! A little over, then down - and full throttle. That's it!

How on Earth can I sit in the middle of all this and think of you, Lulla? It is dangerous, fatal, to think of ANYTHING. Let your thoughts wonder for a split second - and you're dead. Statistics.

I mustn't, I know. And still, I am sitting here, thinking of you, of --.

Have you EVER seen anyone fill your sights like that one there! WOW! Where the hell he came from I don't know - but

I know where he IS! And where he will be in a second. Feel the guns - feel the rhythmic knocking, Lulla!

They're bloody tough these MIGs - take a lot of beating. At least that one. He's being ripped to pieces, but keeps on flying. Trying to escape - twisting, turning, diving, climbing. He's like a frantic eel. Don't let him go - don't let him get away! Stick to him - and fire at the same time, all at over 650 mph.

It's crazy.

Bloody hell! He's gone. Did I get him? No idea, but I don't think so. Damaged, yes. How can anyone tell anything in this? It would be--.

What's it now? It's Jimmy - we're returning.

So - no score today, but two damaged. It's something. Not much, but something. Perhaps I am getting greedy - perhaps I'm beginning to ENJOY all this shooting and killing?

Find your place - then south again.

We didn't lose any today. I am even wondering if they fired a shot at us at all? MIGs are not in a habit of running away, so what happened? All newcomers, do you think?

No idea. And it doesn't bloody matter, does it? We chased them away from the 29s, and that was our task. So task completed.

Full stop.

There are the 29s again. Some of them look in a pretty bad shape. They appear to go fast when you watch them from below; seen from here they look more like they're hanging still; suspended. Going backwards even. As we overtake them, I can see the crew onboard one of them holding five fingers in the air. Five MIGs shot down? Five 29s lost?

Wonder where "Killer" is? Perhaps he's onboard one of them. Would make a change to take a bombing trip one day; find out what it feels like to manoeuvre one of these giants.

Well, no, on second thoughts: no. You can't throw that kite around like we can; you can't twist and turn and dive and climb. You have to keep formation. Steady course before bombs away, steady course, whatever.

No, thanks, I'll stick to this one.

We're soon home again.

"Home" - did I say "home"? - It's much too fast, everything happens too quickly, too fast. This is no "Spirit of St. Louis"! It's development. Development of killing instruments. All because of war. If it's war, nobody asks what the cost is. Money does not matter. A war is like an injection of life into technical development. It's only in peacetime that the pennies are counted and research and development kept on tight reins. The human race owes it technical development to wars. Give us 1000 years with peace, and we'll hardly make any technical advancement at all.

Take the aeroplane. The First World War gave it a slight push forward - a slight push. But not all that much changed between 1918 and 1938. No giant step. No revolution. 20

years.

Then look at the five years - a quarter of the first period - from 1940 to '45! A period when a large part of the world was in flames - then nobody even thought of asking "What's the cost?" The development was staggering.

And afterwards? With Soviet as the big threat and USA as the one who has to counter it, try to stop it, the risk of war, the mere *thought* of war - no question of price.

That's how it is, how it has been - and how it will be. Unless the human being, this supposedly highest of all life on Earth, comes to its senses.

The chances are minute. History, life itself, shows us more than clearly that as long as there are two animals, two people, two living creatures, they will fight each other. Fight each other for dominance, for food, for space, for riches. For anything and everything.

It's simply how we are.

There's the airfield. Jimmy is gliding down, landing - then Billy, Bud --, and I am down. Let it roll a bit, brakes on a bit, - a bit more --, that's it.

Then the trembling again. Reaction. Always after a trip. Always. As certain as the fear before take-off.

It lasts only a moment, OK - evaporating out through muscles and skin. But it's there. Always. Trembling legs, nausea, black dots dancing in front of my eyes. First time it happened I thought I had been injured and was going to die.

Then I prayed to God.

Now I know better.

That's the CO running towards us - better take your picture down - quick! There, in my pocket, next to my heart.

Where you belong, Lulla.

What's up? He's talking - excitedly - to Jimmy. Jimmy checks something in front of him in the cockpit - fuel?

I have 58% left, pressure normal.

Jimmy is scribbling something on a piece of paper, handing it to the CO. What the hell is --?

"Hello, Barnet, hello Barnet - tower calling. Stay where you are - don't leave your planes. Be ready for take-off.

Hello, Barnet leader, Barnet leader - understood? Over."

"Roger." Jimmy was quick.

Surely we're not off again straight away? What the hell is happening? Do they really want us to take off with half the fuel and half the ammunition gone? Either they're going bloody barmy - or it is serious.

I don't know which I would prefer.

The CO is running back, heading for the tower. How long do they want us to sit like --?

"Hello Barnet Red leader, tower calling. Stand by, ready for start. Await orders. Use runway 3. Understood? Over."

"Roger."

Ready for start, he said. Must be something pretty serious

near by. MIGs coming in, perhaps? It may of course be that --
.

There's the signal! But where the bloody hell ARE WE GOING? Say something, someone - for Pete's sake: SAY something!

Jimmy turning, slowling - then off.

Followed by Bobby, Bud, George - and me. Full throttle - stick towards you, not too sudden or hard - gently! There! You're up. Fall in behind - surely someone must say something so we know what the hell --.

"Hello, Barnet Red leader calling. We're meeting some bandits coming in, probably to attack, direction Koypoyang. We may have to turn back before we meet them; we're only covering this area. If they attack another target, we are to return. Follow me - and save fuel!"

So that's it. Enemy aircraft. They rarely attack our bases, but they have shown increased activities lately.

WOW - I have forgotten to put your picture back up, Lulla! - There - that's it. Right in front of me.

"Hello, Barnet Red leader, tower calling. Bandits turning east, turn nine degrees east. Stand by!"

"Roger."

East? Well, then they're not after Kimpo, and if they keep that course for long, we'll have to turn back.

Wonder what's going on north of the border? They are massing enormous forces there, vast amounts of aircrafts and other equipment. Everything points to a major offensive. They have been a lot more aggressive lately. And we are not allowed - NOT ALLOWED! - to attack them. Not north of the border! Can't bomb them - can you believe it! If we don't get rid of these devils, once and for all, what's the point of our boys being maimed and killed - miles from home, in a country they hardly know anything about and care less for?

It is unbelievable - watching them build up enormous forces, sitting waiting for them to attack us, KNOWING they will attack us - and doing sod all about it.

Not allowed! How bloody stupid can you get?

I told you - it is a crazy world. Inhabited by crazy people.

There - I thought so, back to base.

I'm sure Jimmy is delighted - he's going home on extended leave. And he's earned it. He's certainly done his part of the job - AND more.

Look at the village below us. *Village?* I mean the heap of ash and rubble. Not even ruins grinning at you. No life, not even a vague memory of life and how it was. It simply does not seem possible that something - anything - can be so obliterated, levelled, and flattened. Completely. Just dust, ash, and rubble. First the Reds, then our artillery, tanks, and bombs; the Reds' artillery and tanks - followed by our guns and bombs again. Not even tree stumps have been allowed to remain as deathly monuments to our civilzation.

Nothing.

Stick forward. Level out, undercarriage down - there. Easy, easy, relax. Brakes on - a bit more - more, don't hit George. That's it.

That bloody trembling again. What the hell for? We've hardly been away many minutes!

Oh - picture, don't forget it this time! OK. And out.

A-h-h-h - lovely to stretch your legs! They are tight, these 86s. Bloody tight. But you get used to it - you get used to everything in life.

LIFE? HERE?

No, not here. Life is where you are. You and Ian. THAT is where life is.

Not here.

"Will you ring me tomorrow?" What a question! I rang you before 10 in the morning, remember? But your boss said you had just nipped out for a minute. That was enough to make me freeze inside - YOU DIDN'T WANT TO SEE ME AGAIN!

But you rang back ten minutes later - ten LONG minutes. And asked if I wanted to come to a party one of your girlfriends was having that evening.

If I wanted to!

Her name was Mary, you said, and she made the best waffles in the world. Waffles melting in your mouth.

You were probably right - how could I judge anything sensibly with you near me? All I registered, all my senses registered, was that you and I were together.

But I CAN remember that Mary had just bought a brand new radio-gramophone. A large, attractive piece of furniture, in light wood, with a reel-to-reel tape recorder on a shelf on gliders inside. And when you lifted the lid on top, there was the gramophone which could take both 78s and the new LPs - all you had to do was to change the pick-up head. It was the very first time I saw an LP record. I had heard about them and read about them, but never seen one until that evening. Do you remember: we thought it was nearly unbelievable that a record could keep playing for nearly half an hour - compared to the 3 minutes or so we were used to.

That's what we called progress!

And that's where we played "Lavender Blue" and danced. Danced?

I'm sure we were not alone; that all the others were there in the room with us. But since the only light came from that little lamp in the corner, and you held your arms round me and I had my arms round you, you can hardly expect me to remember who or how many were there.

First time "Lavender Blue" had finished you went across to the radio-gramophone and set it so that the pick-up arm moved back and played the same tune over and over again. Do you remember?

And then we danced. Or moved slowly, holding each other tight, kissing.

For a long, long time.

I can vaguely remember that a door or two opened and gently shut - and also that someone, much later, shouted something about turning the bloody record over.

We didn't answer. We didn't bother. All our senses were about each other. Just you and me.

Did someone come in, turning the record-player off - can you remember?

I have no idea. All I remember is that suddenly everything was very quiet.

And we were alone.

When we half sat, half laid on the settee, intertwined, - that's when I told you that I loved you. Told you that all of me, my whole being, just thought about you, dreamed of you, night and day. All the time. You had taken me over - taken over my life, my existence. My world. My world was you.

"Oh, Terry!" you said, and looked at me with those round, beautiful eyes which were always full of smiles.

Always? Not now.

"Oh, Terry!" you said again. "You mustn't!"

I did not grasp what you said, what you meant. Why should I not love you? What was wrong? Why shouldn't I love the most wonderful human being I had ever met?

That's when you told me about Ian.

Ian, doing his national service in the occupation forces in Germany. Ian, whom you had known and been going out with since you were both at school, Ian who regarded you as "his", and whom you had promised to wait for until he finished his national service and came home again.

That's why you hesitated when I asked to see you again.

You liked me, you said - in many ways you liked me more than you liked Ian. Ian had nearly become "a habit" already before he was sent to Germany, you said. Perhaps he had grown to be too sure about it all - started to take you for granted.

"Oh, Terry!" you whispered. "What am I to do? Why do I feel like I do whenever I am with you - whenever we are together? If I *really* loved Ian - I mean *really* loved him with all my heart and feelings - would I feel like I do about you?"

I didn't reply - just I kissed you. Kissed you and held you.

You held onto me as if in despair.

Everything in me had suddenly gone upside-down. Suddenly the world, this wonderful, beautiful world where only you and I existed, was cruelly splintered into a million fragments. I couldn't see you any longer, I couldn't hear you or feel you. You had gone - disappeared with the world.

It was just me left. Alone.

What could I say? What DID I say? Perhaps I did not say anything, uttered no sound, since my brain was paralysed. Frozen to ice. Numbed. Dead.

I might have mumbled something. I don't know.

"I am afraid, Terry - afraid and confused," you said after a while. An eternity. "Afraid that when Ian comes home again, - - I -- . And confused, because whenever I am with you, whenever we are together - I feel so -- so --- FREE, so natural, so happy and relaxed." You laughed, nearly apologetically. "It may sound silly, but how can I explain it? When we are together - I have never felt like this before - I haven't - so - so FREE. Yes, FREE. Happy. Relaxed. I feel ME."

"Do you write to him?" I asked. Or rather, I heard a voice which I presumed was mine asking you.

"Yes. To start with I think we wrote to each other every day. But then --. Now, we write two or three letters a week. But after I met you - and as I have got to know you, I write - I write only because I feel I *should* write, and not because I want to."

You hardly whispered the last few words, but I heard them. I heard them, Lulla!

"Oh, Terry - what SHALL I do?"

Your eyes - those smiling eyes - were full of tears. Tears which trickled slowly down you cheeks. Ever so slowly. Tears I kissed away - without knowing what I should do or say.

"I love you, Lulla!" I said. "Love you more than I can tell you or show you. You have become part of me, your *are* me. Everything I do and think of - it all concerns you. Don't forget that, please, whatever happens."

Did I cry a bit as well? I think so.

"You must believe me, Terry," you said after a while. "Since Ian left I have never, never been out with ANYBODY - until I met you. And I didn't really want to go out with you either. I KNOW I shouldn't have done it. I should have said "No" when you asked me - and stuck to it. I know I should.

But you - there was something about you --. The very few moments, that first afternoon, when you picked up that little book - something I liked. And if only you knew what turmoil my thoughts were in the next day! I said "NO, you mustn't, you MUST NOT meet him tonight outside the office - you MUST NOT!

Only to tell myself the next moment that, well - I could always MEET you - and then not see you again. The second impression might not be as good as the first one, which would make it much easier to say "No" if you asked me out again."

You gave a little smile. Your eyes nearly smiled as well.

I kissed you.

"I am glad you came," I said.

"So am I," you whispered. "You know -- I -- these days we have had together -- if only you knew...."

You broke off, abruptly.

"Oh, Terry! What SHALL I do?"

That was the moment a door opened and someone turned the light on.

We stood a long, long time outside your house that evening. We talked about us - about Ian. Words. Lots of words without meaning, words of no importance. I felt numbed. Confused. Hurt. No, not hurt. Just dead.

"I think it might be best if we don't meet again," I heard you say from somewhere.

Not meet again? NOT MEET AGAIN?!

Did you cut through me with a knife? A rusty, blunt knife?

You did. I felt it. And it was painful.

"We must, Lulla - we MUST!" I felt hollow from fear - fear of losing you. "We can't finish it like this - here, now - tonight! *You* don't want that to happen either!"

This time the tears ran freely down your cheeks.

"No!" you sobbed. "No, Terry, I can't! I can't end it like this either! Oh - TERRY!"

I think the sun was just about to throw its good-morning rays over the hills when we parted, and I caught the first bus of the day home.

Not the last of the day before.

And I felt awful.

It was an attack all right. 27 MIGs attacked some of our boys. A rare occurrence that - so far. But our own aircraft were quickly on the spot and shot down four and damaged three. We didn't lose any. And do you know what, Lulla - it was the 51s which did it! 51s, did you hear? They were the closest and arrived first - and chased the MIGs away before any of the 91s or 86s got there!

See - not a single 51 lost! If only I could get one of those again, a good old real Mustang! They're superb, not only in looks, but beautiful to fly. The bloody speed of these flying stoves may be ideal for catching up a fleeing enemy, but in a battle --! The 51 can out-manoeuvre any of them. Turn on a sixpence.

If only --.

WOW! Would you believe it! We're getting six 51s tomorrow, they say. Six! When the old man asked today if anyone wanted them, well, you should have seen! I think every man stepped forward - at least every man with some experience. You could hardly expect that green youngsters, straight from flying school, bred and trained on jets, have even the slightest notion of how it feels to fly a proper plane, can you?

And I am among the lucky ones, Lulla! I'll be flying a 51 again - a good old fashioned kite with a propeller which goes round and is quite happy with a maximum speed of nearly 440 mph! How's that for luck?

Jimmy very nearly waved goodbye to his leave when he heard the news, "just to fly a proper kite again" as he put it.

Hope we get to try them tomorrow.

***

The enemy has gone on the offensive. A real, full-blown offensive. So far our lines are holding, but for how long? My guess is "not all that long".

Tens of thousands and more tens of thousands of reds flooded down over the border early this morning. It was like a huge dam bursting. They have thrown in aircraft as well, MIG 15 and some Russian Il-3. This is going to be a tough job: up, attack; down again, refilling; up again, attack; down again --. Up - attack - down - shoot, kill.

It's them or us, remember.

We're just about to take off again; just waiting for the orders. The 86s have gone already, it's just six of us left here, six 51s. I am leading today, behind me is Bobby, George, and Ralph, with Sam and Bill making up the rear. They're just like kids at a party; I'm glad to have them here. Reassuring.

I wonder whether we got these 51s simply because a major attack was expected and they wanted to send up to the front everything that could possibly fly, in the hope of being able to stem the offensive? They arrived only a matter of hours before the attack started; given a quick check-up - and made ready in record time.

Must be something really big brewing up North.

There's something homely and friendly about a Mustang. They have personality, a *soul*. Killing machines, I know, but somehow they FEEL different from the 86s.

I wonder if we'll meet any Il-3? There are not all that many of them, as far as we know, and I have never seen them other than on pictures. They're supposed to be extremely dangerous and efficient. "Efficient" here meaning "good at killing" - don't forget that! Kill and murder. That's what it is all about. Nothing else matters.

It's them or us. Either - or.

The Germans called them "Black Death" - that says a lot. Like ours, they've got piston engines, and it --.

Ready? Yes. Right, off we go. It's a pleasure to sit in a 51 again! Like greeting an old friend, familiar instruments --.

Runway 2, he said. There - throttle, increase slowly; careful with the pedals, - a bit more - THERE! Take her up - stick towards you - just feel that, Lulla! A thrilling, pleasant, comforting feeling - I'm airborne in a 51 again!

Strange, isn't it? I always thought these 51s had a hell of a speed: faster, and you would be in trouble. But now --! After the 86s --!

"Hello, Gimlet Red Leader, hello, Gimlet red Leader, Tower calling."

"Hello, Control, Gimlet Red Leader replying. Over."

"Turn three degrees East, follow the road until it crosses the river further North, and attack the enemy on the other side. Don't go too far South-East; the position there is not clear. You'll probably meet the 86s; they have seen quite a few MIGs. Good luck - stand by!"

"Roger."

I don't think we can hold them back - at least not to start with. Not with the masses they have got. It's like holding back a huge army of ants on the march - where do you start? And with the attitude they seem to have to human life - can we cope? Can we in any way accept losses on the same scale as they seem able to, not only to accept, but nearly take for granted?

There's the road.

Wonder if they've crossed the river yet? I'm sure we'll find out.

There it is, the river, a silver-black ribbon far ahead. Better check.

"Hello, Gimlet red Leader calling Control. Can see the river. Over."

"OK, Gimlet red Leader. Carry on."

"Roger. - Hello Gimlet - Gimlet Red Leader calling. Be

damned sure you don't attack our own. Shoot up anything moving or floating on the river. Go low, aim accurately and don't waste ammunition. Rockets only against major targets. Don't spread out too much, concentrate the fire. Look out for bandits!"

The 86s have been here all right. AND done a good job. Smoke and flames all over the place, explosions - all on the North side of the river. I suppose they're waiting until darkness before attempting to cross. It's risky in daylight - risky even for an army heaving in numbers like a huge anthill.

I thought I'd seen a lot, Lulla - but nothing like this. It seems impossible, absolutely impossible, that there can be a single living being, any life, at all down there. All I can see is a chaotic mixture of smoke, explosions, fires - an enormous melting pot of a brew straight from Hell. It's impossible to take it in, impossible to keep up with what is happening down there, up here, all round you. Aircraft, smoke, tracers, sparks, - aircraft rushing towards you, past you, in front of you, above you - everywhere.

The 86s have certainly left their mark. A long convoy of trucks have been converted to a long column of smoke and fire - only interrupted where trucks have been blown off the road, lying like derailed, burnt railway wagons on either side. And there is a --.

Look over there! Artillery firing at our boys further South. What a target!

Stick hard forward - what a feeling to attack with a 51! Splendid aircraft! The ground is rushing towards me, it gets bigger and bigger, filling my whole vision. I can see the gunners quite clearly - they don't even bother about us, they're not looking up or seeking shelter, Lulla! They simply keep on firing, round after round, as if nothing is happening! You can't believe it, can you?

Bloody devils! Just you wait! I'll give you something else to think about than loading and firing, you just wait! There - smack bang in the middle of the sight - press the firing button! The rounds are whipping the ground like water - there! Sweeping straight across the gun position - they're falling, Lulla, they're falling! Closer - CLOSER! DOWN, DOWN!

Not one man left - not one single man left! Did you see that, Lulla? Scattered round the guns like grotesque dolls.

Up again - UP! QUICK! Stick hard back, full throttle - full throttle! Must have been lower than I thought - the trees are stretching their branches out, trying to catch me. One more second - and the ground, the Earth itself - has disappeared. All I can see are clouds, clouds and aircraft. Aircraft everywhere.

The 86s are leaving. They've finished their first round - back to base, refill - and off again.

Bon voyage, boys - you've done a grand job! See you later.

These dives - I feel I am close to passing out when I pull out; black dots dancing in front of my eyes.

Are the others here? I can see three in the mirror - where are the other two? God, I hope they haven't been shot down, please, God - no! Not HERE - not TODAY! Never!

Relax, relax! I'm sure it is Sam and Bill executing some of their private enterprise. Executing! What an appropriate word. That's all we do: execute.

They know damned well that they have to obey orders, stick to the regulations.

Regulations - HERE? There are no rules and regulations here, Lulla. All that's here is murder, killing. Either - or, remember?

It's different where you are. Wonder what you are doing right now? Perhaps --.

What AM I doing, Lulla? Sitting here thinking, dreaming, about you. Here, where letting your thoughts stray for a mere tenth of a second may mean the difference between Life and Death!

Life - HERE?

They're firing at us - oh, no! They've got 88mm guns! Pushed forward with everything they have. As if they didn't have enough already. This will be fun!

Bank a bit and see what --.

I don't believe it! The guns we just finished off have been manned again! They haven't even bothered to clear away their dead comrades - they've simply climbed over them, standing between them and round them, loading, firing, loading, firing --.

Have you ever seen ANYTHING like it? Of course you haven't. Who has? Which normal, decent human being has even been able to *imagine* anything like it? Normal? What IS "normal"? Perhaps this IS normal - and everything else is "abnormal"? Animals kill other animals in order to eat, to survive. Perhaps it is normal for human beings to kill other human beings - not to eat, but to survive? Or simply just to kill? Is THAT "normal", do you think? Perhaps it is peace that's abnormal and against some sort of law of Nature which commands us to kill.

I'll give them manning the guns again! Straight down - down - THERE: fire!

You can't believe it, can you? Just like last time - they're just standing there, carrying on, loading, firing, as if we don't exist.

They're falling - see? Staggering, falling, dropping - only two left. Only one.

There! Nobody left. Just bodies.

Up again- UP! Quick. Any MIGs?

No. Where are they? Why are there no MIGs about? Those poor bastards down there certainly need them here and now!

Never mind - level out, and --! They have manned the guns again! Unbelievable. This is like trying to empty the Pacific with a teaspoon.

But this time - bloody hell, I'll teach them how to man their guns again! One rocket should be enough.

But further down before you send it on its way. The rockets are worth their weight in gold, and you don't waste gold. Although - against this ocean of people and equipment you can hardly miss, can you? Just fire away, you're bound to hit something, somewhere.

There! One should be enough. Can't miss from here.

Those treetops again - closer than I thought.

Climb - fast - and take a look.

Look, Lulla - look! That gun won't trouble our boys any more, that's for sure! Bent, broken, pointing at an angle, the finger of Death has itself died.

The others have done an equally good job - three gun positions blasted off the face of the Earth. Bodies everywhere - some even blown high up into the few trees still standing, looking like grotesque Christmas decorations. The whole riverbank on the north side is more like a carpet of bodies. Or remains of bodies.

I'm glad you're not here, Lulla. This is no place for you.

It's no place for anyone.

Only for Death.

***

The next few days were sheer hell. *Hell*. If you had had merely the slightest idea of how I suffered - suffered all the pains and doubts life and love can possibly muster and throw straight in your face. I won't even try and describe how my thoughts tried to sort out what had happened, what was happening. One moment I was far down in the darkest, most appalling despair - and the next I tried to shake it all off, determined not to be beaten by someone many miles away.

Then all the doubts came again: what could I possibly do? What could I do as long as you loved Ian? Yes, I know, you said you thought you loved me, and I'm sure you meant it. But I was here, with you, and Ian was far away. In Germany. What would happen when he came back home again?

Did I have any right to see you again at all? To be with you? My feelings, my whole body, shouted "YES!YES!YES!," but my brain told me that the only thing to do was for me to pack my bags and stay well away from you.

You and Ian – not you and me - belonged together.

But when heart and brain collide, the result is normally given. The brain rarely wins.

I wandered about as if I were drunk and bewildered. Lifted the telephone - once I even dialled your number - but replaced the receiver immediately.

One day? Two days? Five days? How long was I suspended in this nothing, this empty space? I don't know. I can't remember. Perhaps it was a year. An eternity.

I rang you in the end. In sheer desperation, I think. Just to hear your voice, talk to you, see you in my mind. See you in my mind? Good heavens, Lulla - I had hardly done anything else since we parted!

Your boss answered the telephone, and I very nearly replaced the received again. But I asked for you - and held my breath. My heart was beating so loud and fast that I was sure he could hear it, my hand was shaking so much that it was difficult to hold the receiver against my ear - what would you say? Would you just pass on a message - via your boss - that you did not want to talk to me? That it was all over - finished - forever?

God, was I afraid! Terrified!

Then I heard your voice! Suddenly the sun, the warm, beautiful, life-giving sun, exploded and brushed aside that terrible darkness, and when you said you would like to meet me again that evening -- did I shout? Scream? Gasp? Laugh? Cry? Perhaps all of them. I have no idea.

My death sentence had been annulled. I had been reprieved.

I can't remember all that much of that day or the next few days. They all seemed to merge into a most marvellous intoxication of undiluted happiness, relief, and feeling of walking on air. We were together again, I was with YOU. What else mattered? Everything and anything else was irrelevant.

Ian was never mentioned. That evening was never

mentioned. We were two happy people in love. TWO - because you said---, didn't you? I remember THAT. Not WHEN - but I remember WHERE: in the park. Our park. Where I so very nearly kissed you that first time. And NEARLY by the same tree, but this time we sat on the bench - that wooden bench, painted green, with armrests of wrought iron - remember? Black wrought iron which hurt if you leant against it.

I had my arm round your shoulder. Neither of us spoke. I had no idea what you were thinking, but I was full of happiness. Happiness because we were together again, happiness because I could feel you, the warmth of you, close to me.

That's when you said, without lifting your face, and so softly I could hardly hear it: "Do you know what, Terry. Those days you didn't ring me were some of the worst days of my life. I missed you much more than I have ever missed anyone before."

My heart skipped a few beats - or perhaps it added some extra ones. I can't say.

"Do you mean that?" It was a banal question, I know.

"Yes." And you lifted your face and looked up at me. Even in the yellowish glare from the lamp nearby you looked beautiful.

"But - but what about --?"

You put a finger across my mouth and stopped me.

"I don't know," you said. No, not SAID, you whispered.

As if you were afraid to say it, to admit it to yourself. "I am beginning to doubt that -- I am not sure any longer --. Oh, Terry, what SHALL I do? Sometimes I wish I had never met you, never seen you or heard of you. But why did I miss you so intensely the days you didn't ring? Why did I do nothing else but think of you - think of US? Every time the telephone rang in the office I jumped, I hoped it was you - at the same time as I was frightened. Frightened that it WAS you. Frightened - scared - what might happen if I met you again."

Suddenly the world went into a spin. Round and round like a crazy carousel. Was not this what I hoped for, dreamed of - but never dared to think would ever come true? And whilst everything was still spinning, and before I managed to pull myself together and think of something- anything - sensible to say, your voice penetrated the swirling world inside me. "I love you", it said.

It was two weeks after I rang you again that we went to that radio show, "The Phantoms of the Radio" they called themselves, singing and playing the guitar. We had heard them many, many times on the radio, but never seen them. Until that evening when they came to our town.

It was a great evening, and our hands burnt and ached from all the clapping.

But the next evening was even better - remember?

You had to call in at your uncle and aunt's house that evening. They were away, and you had promised to do something for them. Watering their plants, I think. I may be wrong, but I think that was it. - Anyway, you had to attend to something.

Of course I came along - why not? All I wanted, all I needed, was to be with you. WHERE did not matter. As long as I was with you I was happy. Deliriously happy.

Do you know, Lulla - I can still smell you uncle's house: a warm, cosy, homely smell. A smell may be warm, cosy, and homely.

Yes - that's right - you were watering the flowers. Now I remember. I can even remember the small, green watering can with a long, thin spout. And you were wearing a white blouse and a blue skirt - right? Of course it is right - I can still see you, see you; sense you.

It was when you had finished watering and put the watering can down that you suddenly threw yourself into my arms, clinging to me.

"Terry," you said, and looked at me with those big, blue eyes. "I'm afraid."

"Afraid of what?" What else could I say?

You pressed yourself against me. Hard. Nearly desperate. "I don't know, I don't know. All I know is that I am afraid. Scared. The more we are together, the more I see of you, the more I am doubting. Doubting myself - and Ian --."

"Just wait," I heard myself say, "just wait till he comes home again. Then --."

"No, Terry, no. And perhaps that's why I am so afraid --. This, with Ian --."

You tore yourself away. "You shouldn't have telephoned me again. Never! You shouldn't!"

I think you shouted.

"Never? Suffering like I did? Do you think I could let you go, let you disappear, just like that? And forget you? Whilst everything I did - everything I do, is to think of you, dream about you, want to be with you, day and night?"

I pulled you towards me. You were shaking. Trembling.

Then the tears came. How you cried! You sobbed, the tears running like rivers down your cheeks. I let you cry and cry, let you finish. I could not have stopped you, even if I had wanted to. I just held you, firmly, lovingly, warmly. Held you and let you sob your heart out.

I didn't know what else to do.

"Oh, Terry!" you said after a long while, trying to dry your tears - "I love you - I love you! Don't listen to me when I say you shouldn't have telephoned me -- how I waited for you to ring me! I nearly rang you, many, many times - but how could I? How COULD I possibly ring you and expect you to see me again after what I told you? - Oh, Terry - what SHALL we do?"

I kissed you. And suddenly we were one. You clung to me, hugged me, kissed me with an intensity and wildness - yes, Lulla, wildness! - that literally took my breath away, and pulled me down onto the settee. The world swirled round in a mist again -we kissed and we kissed, I can remember I started unbuttoning your blouse with trembling hands, but you, like me, thought it took far too long time, and we both pulled and tugged and tore it off you, that I remember. But whether I tore your bra off, or you slipped it quickly off, I can't remember.

But your breasts, Lulla - your breasts! Do I remember them! Round, firm, beautiful, and those nipples! You made all sorts of noises when I touched them, squeezed them, kissed them - you wriggled and moved and sighed and were as excited as I was, rubbing against me, at the same time as we both peeled our clothes off, kissing, shouting.

"Take me, Terry - take me! I want you - I want you!" You shouted, loudly. So loudly that for a moment I was afraid they could hear you next door.

But only for a moment.

You didn't have to ask me.

Now, afterwards, perhaps it might all seem -- seem, well, what? A bit helpless? No, not "helpless" - "fumbly", perhaps. I can vaguely remember that in all our excitement we had difficulties in getting our clothes off. Desire and excitement dominated - we trembled and kissed, but finally, finally I slid into you - you had one leg on the floor and the other up over the back of the settee. Good God - why and how do I remember such details?

"Be careful!" you whispered. "Promise you'll be careful!"

When we got our breath and senses back again, we were both on the floor, isn't that right? On the soft carpet with a red pattern.

"It was beautiful," you whispered. "It has never been like that when I -- we -- with Ian --." You hesitated.

"I love you, Lulla, - love you. All I want to do is to make you happy. Take care of you. Love you like you have never been loved before. Never."

Did I believe what you said? Of course I WANTED to believe you - but did I?

We kissed - for a long time. Entwined, close, hot, sweaty, happy, exhausted. Marvellously exhausted.

"This was quite different," you said again. "I gave myself to you, completely, without thinking of anything else. I have never done that with Ian. Believe me, I haven't. Not like this."

And the world span round again. This time from sheer happiness.

I believed you.

To hell with Ian.

It was just the two of us. In the whole world.

And we kissed again.

I think we laid there, on the carpet, for an eternity. Laid there, not saying a word. Just silence. And total peace and happiness, time sliding by.

I asked you if you were sure, quite sure, that your uncle and aunt would not come back that evening. Finding us there, on the floor.

You laughed. That warm, lovely laughter of yours, saying they were not coming back for another two days, and that's why you had to go and water the flowers - "you silly fool!" you added. And kissed me.

We may have dozed off a bit, I can't remember exactly, but gradually and slowly, my hands began to wander over your body again. Caress you. Love you. Touch you. They touched your nipples - only just, but it was as if you received an electric shock the way you reacted. They searched further, stroked - came back to your breasts -- I could feel your slight trembling, I could hear your breathing being faster, - and your hands searched, found - and started exciting me.

And this time it was YOU who rolled me onto my back, remember? You who kissed me, on my mouth, my neck, on my chest - your lips and tongue playing, moving. My body arched - all of it? I can't remember - I was carried away, up, and away, into heaven and above.

And now you were on top, deciding the speed and rhythm, with your irresistible breasts right there in front of me, exciting me even more.

"Be careful!" you said earlier. That was earlier. Now, it was YOU who threw all caution to the wind, it was YOU who went wild, pressing down on me, forcing me so high up into you as was physically possible - you shouted, rolled your head, threw your neck from side to side - your whole body was dripping wet. Wet with perspiration and love juices, wet wet

wet. We shouted and screamed, neither of us able to think, consider, - anything, other than the burning, naked lust and desire for each other.

Then you literally fell off me and heavily onto the floor next to me, your body still shaking as in a spasm, breathing as if you had forced and strained yourself to the utmost and beyond.

Not a word passed your lips, you were drained, empty, apart from some strange noises.

You were beautiful, *beautiful*, your hair a tangled mess. Exhausted. But your eyes said all that had to be said. More than words could.

The most wonderful evening of my whole life.

"Hello, Gimlet Red Leader, Gimlet Red three calling! Aircraft at 2 o'clock - probably bandits!"

Bloody hell! Pull back on stick, throttle - full throttle, climb - gain height - height!

"Hello Gimlet, Red Leader calling! They are bandits OK! Full climb, follow me. Attack first!"

Where the hell have they gone to? I can't see them! Level out a bit - THERE! MIG 15s. Twelve - FOURTEEN of the bastards - and we are six! Six 51s. Piston against jet - manoeuvrability against speed.

We're just above them. Better split in two and try and get them from behind and side.

"Hello Gimlet, Gimlet Red Leader caling. Red follow me

on starboard, the rest takes care of port. Be sure you have them in your sight before letting go!"

Bobby is with me. Poor Bobby, he is far to young for this - a mere boy. Hardly shaving yet --. But he's brave. Very brave.

They are separating. Into three groups. What the hell are they thinking of, splitting into three? Never mind - let's take the starboard one. They're climbing - fast. Push forward - take the one in the middle. THERE! Give it all you have! Down - faster -throttle!

The others are peeling off, out and up. A climbing speed we can't match - that's for certain. Keep your eyes off them - take that bastard you've got in your sights! Stick to him, STICK TO HIM, I say! DON'T LET HIM GO! Just keep firing - even he can't take everything.

There - see, Lulla? He's diving - as good as vertically. But don't be fooled, it's only evasive action. He's not finished. After him! - NO, WAIT! That's just what he wants you to do, you bloody fool: follow him, forgetting everything else, only for one of his bloody friends to finish you off! Break off - BREAK OFF! UP - fast!

THERE - in the mirror! A MIG right behind you - quick - QUICK - rudder, pedal --, PFUII! He shot past. That was a close one! Couldn't turn on a sixpence like a 51! What did I say?

Suddenly the sky is full of aircraft forming a chaotic pattern. Crossing each other, chasing each other; diving, climbing, spiralling. How the hell can anyone - ANYONE -

keep track of what is what and who is who in this lunatic dance of men and machines? Just fire away - you seem bound to hit something or somebody, that's how intermingled it all is.

Hit something or somebody. Either - or.

That was Sam shooting past with one on his tail. And there's Bill. They are certainly sticking together!

There - look! At 11 o'clock! He's just above me - with a bit of luck I'll get him right in his dead-angle of vision - THAT'S IT! Full throttle - don't get so high that he sees you! Careful.

Bloody hell - he's turned away! Down - down - away - LEVEL OUT! Has he seen you? No, he's after George. Concentrating on George, not looking.

That's his mistake. One mistake - that's enough. You rarely get a second chance here, Lulla. One slight mistake, and that's it.

And he's just made his.

Did you say hits? He can feel them - but he has no idea where they're coming from. Twisting and turning - NOW he's seen me, but now is too late: he should have dived straight away, without spending precious tenths of a second looking round, trying to find out where I was.

Perhaps he had no choice. Perhaps my first round hit him, and it was the aircraft twisting and turning on its own, before putting the nose down, straight down, leaving a trail of flames and smoke.

Does it matter? It bloody well doesn't!

All that matters is that there's one bastard less.

Look out - the mirror! A MIG right behind you again!

Left pedal quickly forward, stick forward; right rudder, and back again on the stick - is he still there?

No! As I thought, no way these blasted flying stoves can turn like that! Not with such small wings and with that speed.

Bobby is behind him. Hope he gets him.

What the hell is that? That noise in -- IT'S HITS! HITS IN MY PLANE!

BUT WHERE FROM?

No idea - just dive - DIVE! Fast - FASTER - full throttle - GET OUT OF HERE!

He's still there - I'm not enjoying this --, turn, turn fast, shake him off! Then climb, steep, fast.

Bloody hell, he's still there, the bastard! Loop - LOOP and see if he can manage --.

HE DIDN'T, Lulla, and *now I'm behind him!* Behind the bastard. No way could he loop as tight as that. See?

I'll pay you back. With interest. THERE! Look at his tailfin, Lulla - just look at it! A circular saw wouldn't have done a better job.

That was one of his friends cutting straight across him, forcing him to lift his nose a bit - enough to fill the whole of my sight. Thanks, Comrade! That's all I needed. See - he's jumping, Lulla - he's jumping!

That's two today, TWO MIGs! What did I say about the

51s? 51s and Spits? Yes, well, I know - I got a helping hand from one of his comrade friends with this one, but still. You need a bit of luck now and then.

A BIT of luck? A bloody great bucket full of luck!

"Gimlet Red to Gimlet Leader. Engine damaged, I'll try and put her down south of the river. Think I'll manage. Make an 86 ready for me!"

Bobby hit! Why doesn't he jump? Why? Would you bloody jump here, on the north side of the river?

You bloody well wouldn't!

Bobby is so young - he must make it - he MUST. Please!

"Hello Gimlet Red Leader, Barnet Red Leader calling."

Its Frank! The 86s are back!

"Hello Barnet Red Leader - Gimlet Red Leader here. Over."

"Hello, Gimlet - looks like you've done a great job. You can go home, we'll take over."

"Roger."

Just as well - not much ammo and fuel left. Too easy to forget about all this in the middle of all the excitement. I know you shouldn't, not supposed to - but then: you do. Simple as that. You do.

Call them all back - there.

Where's Bobby? Can't see him, he should be roughly --. YES, THERE HE IS! Gliding gently down, smoke coming from his engine - it's as if he's drawn his descent with a grey pencil. Why doesn't he jump, now he's well clear of the river? With all that smoke -- a sudden flame - an explosion --. He's only 19. 19! What an age to die. No, he mustn't - he can't - he MUST get her down. But what happens if he can't find a flat piece of land - just mountains and trees? Black, charred, sharp stubs!

We are five - with one damaged. If only Bobby makes it, we're still six! The 51s did it, they got the job done. - Back to refuel, - then up again. Up again to kill some more. It's easier from up above, from a distance. It's as far from hand-fighting as you can get. Detached. You just press a button and destroy machines. That's all.

It's frustrating landing with some of the rockets intact, but these bloody MIGs ruined the whole thing. But at least we got some of them - I don't know how many, but some. I got two - TWO! Would you believe it, Lulla!

We're still holding the south bank, but for how long can we resist this ocean of human beings, a flood wave the world has never seen the like of, swamping everything in its path? The sheer weight of it, the masses, the enormity, makes it seemingly impossible to stop or even slow down. And yet, we must, Lulla, we must. Somehow. If not --.

"Hello Gimlet Red Leader - Tower calling. Over."

"Gimlet Red Leader here. Over."

"Use Runway 3, taxi to West hangar. Wind force 17. How are things? Over."

"Nobody missing - but Bobby is damaged. Would try to get her down, he said - I'm sure you heard it. Last I saw him he looked OK, but trailing smoke. We got some guns and some MIGs. I received some hits, no idea where, but all seems normal. Over."

"OK. Stand by."

I can hear Frank giving orders. They've got a lot to do today. A lot to keep them occupied. And so have we. A lot to do. Many to kill. Many to exterminate.

It's a great world.

There's Kimpo. It's a marvellous feeling to glide down in a 51 again, Lulla. A marvellous feeling. A beautiful aircraft.

Wheels down? Everything OK? Right - nicely down, roll forward . What did he say: West hangar? Yes, - there we are.

It's far more comfortable – "comfortable", HERE, in all this? What a joke! - with a 51 than an 86. At least you have time to register what rushes past you. A chance to think and react.

That's it - relax. Don't forget to take the photo down!

There's that blasted trembling again. Every time I have landed, this blasted trembling. "Reaction" I think they call it. Call it what you like, it comes. Every time. Without exception.

The fitters are already running towards us - and there's the tanker. No time to lose here, away again as fast as possible. Away - to kill more. To numb senses and human feelings. No excuses! It's them or us. Remember: either - or.

Better walk over to the tower to see if they've heard anything from Bobby.

***

We talked about spending the night there, didn't we? On the settee - on the floor - it did not seem to matter. Just lie there, make love, talk a bit, sleep a little, be close, very close, to each other, and make love again.

I suppose you were quite right when you said we'd better go home; to go straight to the office from there, next morning.

It was past 3 in the morning when we rang for a taxi for you. And as you said, it was pointless for me to see you home, to the other side of the town, only to have to turn round and go back the same way, more or less.

I lived not far from your uncle and aunt, so I walked home. That's all I am able to remember. That I walked home.

But *straight* home? Or did I walk around in a glorious haze of happiness? That I can't remember. My brain, head, thoughts - everything was spinning. The entire spectrum of what a human being can feel and experience and think swelled through me: elation, exhaustion, delirious happiness, confusion, bewilderment, intense tiredness, and a sudden and great faith in the future. It was all there, filling my whole body, head, soul, limbs. Not in a neat and orderly fashion, but all at once. On top of each other, stirred and mixed together.

How could I possibly keep cool and be level-headed? You, Lulla, the girl I loved, the girl who had literally and in every way taken over my life, all of me, had given me the most wonderful, most beautiful, and most exciting evening I could possibly imagine or desire.

Is it strange that I have no idea when I got home - or how I got home, other than the fact that I walked?

My wildest dreams were suddenly a reality - and WHAT a reality!

You were mine. I was yours.

Us. Just the two of us.

Of course I rang you the next day - or later that day, rather. In the evening we saw a film, "In old Chicago". That's all I remember. What it was about, who was in it, it has all been deleted from my memory. I remember the name of the film - and that YOU sat next to me; that we held hands and that we walked in the park - our park- afterwards.

How much more do you expect a fellow in love to take in?

We stopped every tenth step and kissed. Held tight, and kissed. A long time. We sat down on OUR bench - you did not say much, and I asked if there was something wrong.

That DOUBT again! The doubt which I thought the evening before had banned into oblivion, once and for all.

But it came back. Suddenly like a cold, ice-cold, hand, gripping me inside.

Simply because you didn't talk much; seemed far away.

You shook your head.

"It's - I'm just thinking -- I don't know --."

I put my hand under your chin, lifting your head, afraid of the answer.

"What IS it, Lulla? What's the matter?"

"Do you think -- do you think something happened last night?"

Something happened? Of course something happened! The most wonderful evening --.

Suddenly I grasped what you meant, Lulla, and the ice-cold hand melted away. So THAT was it!

"No," I said. I didn't lie, Lulla. I didn't KNOW either, but somehow --.

"But -- but - that second time, when I was on top, are you sure -- sure that --nothing happened?"

"I don't KNOW, but I am pretty sure."

"You were wonderful!" you whispered. "I have never felt it like that before. Never. I gave myself completely to you, Terry - completely. There was nothing in me holding back, nothing. You made me feel so -- so FREE, so relaxed --." You stopped, then smiled a bit. "I think I've said that before!" you said.

"You may say it again. And again. And again. A thousand times. I'll kiss you every time you say it."

And I did.

It was the next evening, when I came round to pick you up, you suggested I should come in and meet your mother. And if it is true what they say, that if you want to see what your girlfriend will look like in 20 or 40 years' time, take a look at her mother, you've certainly got something to look forward to, Lulla! She was every bit as attractive and charming as you, just as cheerful, - and with the same laughing eyes and little dimples. A bit rounder, true, - but still having a figure which would turn the heads of most men.

And what she said, Lulla - what she SAID - when you introduced me to her, made my heart jump and skip wildly.

"Very nice to meet you," she smiled – "Lulla hasn't done much else lately than talk about you."

Not done much else! Than talk about me!

Did I blush? Did I stutter and get all embarrassed?

It was certainly more than sufficient to throw my brain and thought into a spin again, from sheer happiness. If I appeared absent minded as we sat there chatting for a while, it was because I was absent minded. How could anyone expect me to concentrate on small talk and polite conversation after your mother, YOUR mother - had just told me that you hadn't done much else than talk about me lately? Angels filled the room, and I heard soft, beautiful music - not voices.

And more angels and more music filled the world the next day, when I met you outside your office, and you said your mother liked me.

"He seemed a real nice chap," she had said. "You must hold onto him!"

Hold onto!

It is *I* who have to hold onto *You*, Lulla!

We're being pushed backwards and southwards. I never knew such masses of people even existed, let alone could be concentrated in such a relatively small area of the World. And the attitude! Totally foreign, totally abhorrent to our way of thinking, difficult to imagine, impossible to understand: some of our 86s came across some Chinese marching south, and attacked them. The soldiers didn't even stop, seek shelter, - anything - they just kept on marching as if nothing was happening! Like lemmings. Stepping over their dead comrades. Marching - marching. Our boys couldn't believe it!

And this is what we are fighting against - this is what we are trying to stop.

We're off in a minute, they're working on Billy's plane. We haven't heard anything about Bobby yet, we're just hoping. Hoping he made it OK. If only he found a fairly level place to put her down, he should --.

Did I get a bit of a shock when I looked more closely at my plane! Three holes – one very, very close to one of the petrol tanks, and one too close to the control wire for comfort. It would have been more than exciting with a burning plane, completely out of control. As it is, there's no danger, so I am off again with the others.

Sam is in a bit of a mess - or his 51, rather. On an ordinary day they would no doubt have grounded him until it had all been repaired, but when the old man mumbled something along those lines, Sam brushed him aside and said that

President Harry S could ring him - Sam - personally and ground him, and he - Sam - would tell Harry S to go to hell.

The old man smiled and said that, well, Truman would probably not telephone, so it was OK with him.

And Bill agreed.

So here we are. Five aircraft. Five aircraft being thrown in to help stem the Masses. And I mean Masses. If only we had been fifty - or five hundred, but FIVE!

Well, we'll do our bit - take a bite here and take a bite there.

We're off further west this time. The Reds have managed to breach our lines and are streaming through. We're throwing at them all we have - masses of aircrafts; our 86s are on the way back here for refuelling - and then off after us.

There - the signal.

Quick, everyone up. EVERYONE? There's only FIVE of us, for Heaven's sake!

Five aircraft. It must look a bit comical, pathetic even, to see these five dashing up and forward, like five mosquitoes attacking a swarm of swallows; five mice throwing themselves at thousands of cats --.

Five aircraft!

Can we win this war? Or is everything we do in vain - a total waste of lives, efforts, materials? Will what we do contribute to a better world, a free world? Can we win, once and for all, and show the world that freedom is stronger than imprisonment and torture; show people that if only the world, the FREE world, wants to, then we can win against tyrants, dictators and slavery, against crazy ideas and ideologies?

We have discussed it many a time. Ash was convinced we could. He was a good one - too good, too kind, too understanding. The most decent chap I ever knew, I think. He believed deeply and sincerely in people's right to a free choice, a democracy where the majority was guided by the wishes and needs of the minority. There was no doubt in his mind that if we could only get rid of oppression, whether it was called nazism or communism or something else, the world would be a better place. A good place. A free place. He saw people as basically good and kind and considerate and tolerant - except tolerant with regard to oppression and tyrants.

He regarded the United Nations as the one thing the world needed to end wars and conflicts. A strong United Nations would be the best guarantee that no country would even think about attacking another.

Bobby agrees with him in a way. But only in a way. His first and only aim is to revenge his father - kill as many reds as he possibly can. Will the world be better for it? He shrugs his shoulders and says he doesn't care - but *he* will be. A lot better.

Frank agreed with Ash and is in no doubt that once we get rid of this cancer, we will all live in peace and harmony. "The last obstacle to peace - real peace," he calls it. And he is determined we will win. Win or disappear. As simple as that. Either - or. That's all there's to it.

Perhaps it is. It would be nice to think so. But if you're realistic and look at history, will we ever be able or even willing to abolish war, just like that? How? Where do you start? Even if Europe becomes a "United States of Europe", which to my mind is absolutely necessary if we are to have any chance of avoiding wars in Europe in the future, will it help?

Only as a first step, as a first "Union". We have to take USA as an example: 48 individual and fully independent states would without doubt NOT have been able to exist in harmony; wars between two or more of them would simply have been inevitable. But how can Europe possibly be expected to unite like the US? True, USA has probably people from as many - if not more - countries and different backgrounds than Europe, all with their own cultures, habits, and customs. But they threw it all into the melting pot, creating a new nation. Something Europe won't be able to; which country will be willing to say goodbye to hundreds, even thousands, of years of history and tradition? You can't forget that overnight - you can't forget your old heroes who beat your neighbours into the dust.

And to be ONE, you need ONE currency - can you imagine USA with each of the 48 states having their own currency? - and more or less one, a single taxation system, with only minor variances for each country within the overall system.

Europe ONE?

A pipedream, perhaps. And yet: if the dream does not come true, we won't make any progress on the road to peace and coexistence. We have to build larger units, as it were, for the simple reason that history shows us very clearly that two independent countries, large or small, in all probability will sooner or later clash and go to war against each other, whilst two states, forming part of a larger Union, won't or can't. Which means that the ultimate aim and only hope of survival is a "United States of the World". It will require statesmen, and not mere politicians.

Some dream! Some task!

Oh yes, we have discussed it. Many times. But can we *really* make any difference? Perhaps not. The most we can do is probably to prevent any more countries from being swallowed by evil; whilst the countries already under the communist yoke can only be freed from within. They will have to do it themselves. But even then: how far can - how far *should* - we go? If, say, the Baltic republics revolted tomorrow, should we send in planes and soldiers to help - and probably trigger the Third World War, with all its terrible consequences? The dividing line between "help" and "interference" is fine indeed.

No empire lasts forever. Even the Roman empire disappeared - an invincible Empire if ever there was one.

When it comes down to it: perhaps it's just a mere question of time, and all our efforts and sacrifices are totally useless, stupid, and in vain. Who knows. Who the hell knows anything?

There are the 86s. A hell of a speed. Bloody fast. But in a fight, when the ability to turn and manoeuvre quickly is most important in my opinion --. Two - *three!* - are missing! Shot down? Damaged? Who are they? No time to look properly - no time to any damned thing in all this. Glad Jimmy is not here.

Down there, below us - our boys are moving north. Towards the front. Fresh reinforcements. They're waving to us - to five of us. Waving! As if they're on a school outing and we're giving them a little display! If I had been down there I would have been scared out of my wits. Terrified. Even more than I am before we take off. Perhaps they are, for all I know. And they keep marching.

"Hello Gimlet Red Leader, control calling."

"Gimlet Red Leader answering. Over."

"Bobby has reported he's OK - landed in a field. Coming as soon as he can - he has demanded that another plane is waiting for him, ready to take off! The 86s are off again in a minute. Frank says "Good luck. Over.""

"Thanks, Tom. Glad to hear Bobby is fine. Tell Frank we'll leave some work for him to do - over and out."

Frank. That means that he's not one of those missing. Good.

There are the guns. They've crossed the river in one place. We are not after any definite targets; just shoot up and destroy. Kill - Kill as best we can. As many as we can. There's plenty to choose from.

Things have changed here. Now, below us, our boys are moving south. Tired, exhausted, dispirited I should think. Vehicles, people in what looks like a chaotic mass from up here, on their way to take up new positions. "Tactical retreat" it is called, isn't it?

Some poor bastards are staying behind, delaying the enemy to give the others more time.

And there - over there - some of our 29s. They have undoubtedly been further north, and now on the way back to fill up. Like the rest of us: no rest. Keep going. Keep killing.

LOOK AT THAT! What a target: three boats in the middle of the river, full of soldiers! Let's make sure they never reach the south bank!

"Hello Gimlet, Gimlet Red Leader calling. Let's take the boats down there in the middle of the river. No rockets. Go ahead!"

Down - straight down - straight at them. I think they have heard us through all the noisy, boiling inferno surrounding them. They have heard us - the whine of five little planes diving towards them - five executors intended to execute every single one of them. Efficiently - but not necessarily painlessly!

Why the hell don't they jump into the river and at least *try* to get away? Surely they must realise that THEY are the target - and a bloody good target at that? Jump, you stupid bastards - jump!

But no, they're not even taking evasive action - just heading in a straight line. A line straight out of this world and into the next.

They're getting bigger and closer. Fast. And only a handful of them are even looking up. I can see their faces quite clearly - blank faces just staring. But most of them don't pay us the slightest attention, staring only straight ahead - towards the south bank.

South bank. They'll never reach it!

There's about 50 men in each boat, I should think.

NOW! Ra-ta-ta-ta --. The rounds are whipping the water into foam, drawing angry lines towards, across and over the boat. They are falling - falling, some overboard, others on top of their comrades. But the boats carry on - just carry on.

It's not long ago, Lulla, that a sight like this would have made me feel sick. Ill. Guilty. Ashamed. But now?

It is frightening. It's not much different from aiming at targets on a firing range. I have no feeling of sitting in a murder machine, killing and maiming young boys - human beings. I don't even give it a thought. Young boys like myself. Boys with a home and family, and friends. Perhaps even children. But not only don't I give it a thought, Lulla - perhaps worse is the fact that far from feeling unwell, ill, and terrible like a "normal" person would feel by the mere thought of sending hundreds of bullets ripping into living flesh, killing - I nearly feel some sort of sick pleasure from it all, a tingling excitement from seeing the result of my actions.

Is this the effect war, killing, murder has on people, Lulla? Is this the height, the pinnacle of civilisation? The end result of all our talents and abilities? Making sure that our boys on the ground have 150 or 1500 fewer enemies to take care of?

To hell with such soft thoughts! Remember: it's either - or!

Not further down now - back with the stick, round - and down again. One of the boats is sinking, so what? Give it another round - there's still people onboard. Living humans to be converted into dead humans.

Conversion. That's what I'm doing.

The river is rushing towards me again. The boat is smack bang in the centre of my aim - NOW! There won't be many left after that, I can tell you! Not many at all, Lulla! Keep it steady - steady. See how they're falling? Falling, toppling overboard, sinking --. And there - the boat disappears!

Up again - level out - look around!

Any MIGs about?

Why aren't there any? Where are they? Why haven't they swarms of them up here, protecting their comrades down there, preventing us from picking them off like the sitting ducks they are.

Where ARE the MIGs, Lulla?

It's all very odd.

"Gimlet Red Leader calling Gimlet! That's enough, guys. Increase height and look for new targets."

There's still five of us - Bobby is OK. So far we've kept our debit side blank. But for how long can we --?

"Hello Gimlet Red Leader - Gimlet Red 3 calling. Look at the road north-northeast - troops, I think."

North-northeast - let's see -- yes, bloody hell! I'll say that's troops! The road is spilling over as far as you can see with soldiers and equipment heading south.

"Hello Gimlet, Red Leader calling. Attack the troops, go in low and use the guns. Rockets if necessary, but no more than two."

Turn slightly, and down. Take the column from one end to the other. Guns only. Just above treetop height - that's it! The soldiers are getting bigger and bigger - normal infantry. But nobody is seeking shelter, they keep on marching, marching, straight ahead, ignoring us completely.

There are only five of us.

NOW! I am hardly thirty feet above their heads - they don't even LOOK UP, Lulla! Soldiers, soldiers, soldiers as far as I can see. The whole width of the road. For a second I wonder if I am looking at ants or people. It is simply impossible to miss - the chatting guns are whipping and ripping into the mass rushing past and underneath me - I have never seen or heard anything like it, Lulla. You can't believe it, I am sure. Nor could I had I not seen it. And even then --.

Now - up, turn, down and round again. The other four are

following.

Good God - what a sight! I am glad you are not here, Lulla, and I am glad I cannot describe it to you. It's the most awful, dreadful sight I have seen in my life - the empty spaces, left by the dead and dying, immediately being filled by the others, stepping over the bodies in their way - marching, marching southwards. Like robots. Machines. Marching as if we don't exist. An ocean of human beings on the move. What can we possibly do to stem up such a tide, Lulla?

Let go two rockets - two rockets into the moving, heaving mass of human bodies. No need to take aim - just let the damned things go. Like that!

See what I mean?

What a bloodbath! What a massacre! And still they keep going, steadily, unstoppable.

I can't believe it.

One more round, with the guns. The whole thing is unbelievable. No, worse - far worse than simply unbelievable. It is beyond any civilised comprehension. We are not fighting human beings, Lulla! We are fighting indoctrinated, programmed robots, and not human beings, with feelings, thoughts, hope, joy, sadness, like you and me. People made from flesh and blood.

It is unreal. Incomprehensible. Not even a Hollywood film could possibly have portrayed this. Simply because no human being could possibly have thought of or imagined it.

Over - up, turn, and in again. Do you see, Lulla - there are so many dead bodies in the way that those behind have difficulties climbing over them or walk round them, leaving gaps in the column. Have you ever seen anything like it, Lulla? No, of course you haven't, - nobody has. Perhaps we CAN succeed after all. Surely there must be a limit even to what they can endure?

AT LAST! They're seeking cover! Reluctantly it seems from here. Off the road and in among the trees.

It's nearly a relief.

It IS a relief!

Which only goes to show the lunacy of this war. Not only this war, but all wars. War is lunacy. Human lunacy.

Do animals have wars? They fight, yes - but WARS? Perhaps the animals are the higher order - without us humans realising it?

The next days, weeks - or was it months? - no, not months! - were the happiest, sweetest, best of my whole life. Because of you. Because I was with you. We were together.

And you were as happy as I was, weren't you, Lulla? That, at least, is what your eyes told me, told the world. Those beautiful eyes never stopped sparkling, smiling, laughing. And I inhaled it all - inhaled and absorbed everything about you. Everything. All of you. You filled me with you and full and total happiness.

I was in the seventh heaven - and still ascending.

What we did? EVERYTHING!

It's easier to say what we DIDN'T do!

We went to the cinema, of course. Quite often. "Harbour lights" - I remember that one because you liked the main tune so much that I tried to buy the record for you, but in vain. I asked in every record shop - I virtually pleaded with them to get the record, but it was no good. They might well have had the record on sale in America, but certainly not here. Two shops tried to sell me another one, "equally good", as they said. Equally good? It had to be "Harbour lights" - or nothing. What does "equally good" mean? It either is - or it isn't.

See, Lulla, even then - in those exactly happy days, it was "either - or"?

But the films we saw were not important - what was important was that we were together. We held hands. We laughed together and we felt the warmth and the happiness flow through us. I held you tight in my arms, we kissed - we made love, we explored each other.

Like that Sunday we went for a walk in the mountains.

You had your sporty outfit on; a small white-and-blue knitted hat with a tiny tassel, and old, brown windcheater which did its best to hide your very feminine forms but made a hash of it, contrary to your tight-fitting skiing pants which very much succeeded in emphasizing them.

WOW!

I was convinced that the world - not to say The World - turned round and looked at me with envy as we walked along, hand in hand up the gravel track snaking its way to the top.

It was a beautiful day. EVERY day with you was a beautiful day, so let me put it like this: the sky was blue, the sun was shining and the wind stayed at home, and we were together. Close together.

We followed a path through the pine forest - we skipped and danced between the trees, played a lovers' form of hide and seek, stopped, kissed - skipped some more, chased each other round and in between the trees - stopped, embraced, and kissed some more.

Did we meet other people? Did we see anyone? Don't ask me - I have no idea. If we did, I did not notice. All that my senses registered was that you were there. Next to me. We were together. And alone in the world.

Just you and me.

I know we definitely did not see or hear anyone when we stumbled across that little hut, or cabin, or whatever you would call it. It had been built in a clearing in the forest, well away from any roads or paths, and had probably served as a scout hut or sports club's hut at one time. But that was many years ago, more than likely in the 30s. Now, it was a ramshackle old thing with gaping holes where the windows used to be, and what was left of the door was hanging at an angle, precariously held by one hinge. Some boards where missing from the walls - and inside was just dust and rubbish.

In front of the hut, on the south side, warmed by the sun, was a large, flat stone. Or part of the mountain itself, I should think. Do you remember? You took off your windcheater, and I took off mine, making them into cushions we could sit on.

That light blue jumper you had on! Little wonder the windcheater didn't have a hope in hell of hiding your shapely forms.

Come to think of it, we didn't so much have "cushions we could sit on" as "cushions we could lie on"---. If my memory serves me right we were lying flat out, tightly embraced and kissing before we had time to fully regain our breath after the climb, and one of my hands found one of your breasts, then the other one, before it crept under your jumper and found your firm and very exciting and excited nipple.

You twisted your body away a little, and put your hand on my arm and pushed it down. Not too hard, but down.

"No, please," you said. SAID? No - you SIGHED, deep - and you trembled. I could feel you trembling, as if you were cold. "No, please - not here."

You didn't seriously believe I could or would stop? No more seriously so than I thought you really meant it! Didn't all of you - your whole body, your eyes - shout: "TAKE ME! TAKE ME! I AM YOURS - AND YOURS ONLY!"

That's why I did not listen to your voice, to words I knew full well you did not mean. Instead, I did what your eyes, your mouth, your breathing told me you wanted me to do - and they all contradicted your words.

That's why I did not stop.

"Not here!" you said again, now more faintly, weaker. Even less convincing.

"What's wrong with here?" I asked, and this time you did not push my hand away.

"People - people might come --." It was just like a whisper.

"Here?" I said. "Miles away from anywhere? People never come here!"

"But *we* did," you said, logically enough.

But logic had nothing to do with it. Not there and then. Not when we were together. Feelings, yes. Logic, no.

It wasn't long before you whispered it was too hard to lie on the stone, even with two windcheaters between you and the stone - so we dragged ourselves into the grass and heather.

If anyone had suddenly appeared - would we have noticed

them? For all I know, half the town's population might well have strolled past on their Sunday outing, spotted us, rolled their eyes towards the Heavens - and hurried on, pretending not to notice.

I don't know, and neither do you.

But I do know that to love you in that way, among prickly heather, with the blue sky as nearest ceiling and the sun streaming down, warm and cosy, was a totally new experience. A new, exciting experience. As if we needed something new and exciting!

We laid there, a long time, afterwards, side by side. Exhausted, utterly, totally happy and exhausted.

"Do you know, Terry," you whispered, "you make me feel - experience - things I have never, ever experienced or felt before. This is the first time I really exploded inside - very different and far, far better than anything I have known or could even imagine. - I thought for a moment that my whole body was going to be torn apart."

You lifted your head and looked at me: "I love you, Terry. Perhaps I shouldn't do, but I can't help it. I love you and need you."

It was not until we heard voices - only just, but voices! - that we were pulled so brutally back into this world and managed hurriedly to rearrange our clothing to some sort of decent order and sit on the stone as if we had just paused in our walk to have a little rest. When the elderly couple had walked by, after giving us a nod and a smile, you blurted out: "What if they were here a little while ago - discovered us, withdrew quickly, and waited a little before walking on?" And we both laughed and kissed again.

It was when we sat there talking that I suddenly realised how little I really knew you. A fact which had never bothered me the slightest, nor had I ever left it a single thought. You were the most wonderful girl in the world - you were simply the most wonderful person I had ever met, the girl of my dreams; always smiling, always happy, always YOU. What more could I want?

It was plenty enough for me.

But when we sat there, and you started talking about plants and shrubs and flowers, and pointed to some small, yellow flowers nearby and said what they were called, I got very surprised at first. I don't know why, but I did. I can think of no earthly reason why I should get surprised at you knowing the name of some flowers. Perhaps it was just that we had never *talked* about things like that before.

And you knew the various birds, both from their singing and their shape. Well, yes, of course, I could tell the difference between a magpie and a sparrow if I saw them close up, but the lot in between --, no, not really.

It was there, on top of that mountain, in front of the old hut about to collapse completely, blissfully happy and utterly, totally exhausted in body but not in mind, that I REALLY got to know you.

We sat there, leaning against each other, in Paradise, in warm sunshine, the air still and clear, a beautiful view over the town. Just the two of us in the whole, wide world.

And without me asking or prompting you, you started to tell me about yourself. About how you had spent most of the War-years on a farm, run by your mother's cousin, far far away from towns, cities, war, and strict rationing. Your father and mother stayed behind in town, together with your older sister and brother because of their schooling, but spent all holidays at the farm.

That's where you learned about the various birds, flowers, plants, bushes, and trees - about nature. You could tell the difference between a kestrel and a buzzard in flight, you said, and added: "And *that's* something which is a great advantage here in the town!," and laughed. That happy, contagious laughter which always lit up your eyes, making them shine and sparkle even more than usual.

And it was there, in the sunshine, on top of the mountain, you told me about life the way it should not be. You did not complain, you did not accuse anybody, you only talked - opened yourself, described it the way you had experienced and seen it. And felt it. How, after the War, when you came back to town, your father stunned you all by suddenly and completely unexpectedly announcing that he had found "someone else" and was moving out and leaving you all the next day. The "someone else" was a secretary in the bank where he worked. He told you they had already bought a flat on the other side of the town, and there was no point discussing anything at all. It was all decided, and there was no way back.

Your mother could not believe it. None of you could believe it. In a matter of a mere second the world and life as you had known it disintegrated to dust and disappeared. For weeks and months afterwards you were in a daze, - all your confused and bewildered minds could manage to say was "Why? WHY?"

And as you gradually and slowly began to recover, life began to take some shape and form again, feeling perhaps stronger and closer as a family, your brother was killed in an accident at work.

That was nearly three years ago, you said, but it felt like it was yesterday.

Your sister had married shortly before it happened and moved far away, so you were the only one left to look after and support your mother.

"That's why, Terry," you said so softly I could hardly hear it — "that's why I say, feel, that I have to be early home so often. It is not because I don't want to be with you - because I do - but I can't leave mother alone, night after night, thinking, missing, feeling that terrible emptiness and nothing. I am all she has got - here.

You understand me, don't you?"

Oh Lulla! You are pretty and attractive; not only when you are laughing and smiling, but also when you are crying. When the tears are streaming freely down your cheeks.

Which they did now. And you crept closer to me, you held me as if you were afraid that I would push you away.

ME? Push you away?

What could I say? What DID I say?

I have no idea. I can't remember. Probably something feeble like "Poor Lulla!"

"Mother likes you," you continued and dried your tears. "She really likes you. I know she's only met you once, - but she is a good judge of people."

Your head rested against my shoulder, my arm tight and safely round you. Neither of us spoke for some time - a long time, perhaps. We just sat, you leaning against me, I holding you. A bird suddenly shrieked and fluttered hurriedly into the air, obviously startled by something.

"Mother - she --." Your voice trailed off, died. You hesitated. I think I said "Yes?" - and waited.

You lifted your face and looked at me. Your eyes were red and wet, but you had stopped crying.

"Mother does not like Ian very much. She never has done. I don't know why, but she doesn't. She says - she says that I should forget about Ian and hold on to you.

Oh, Terry - TERRY! Don't you understand - I am

confused, frightened. I don't know what to do. I don't what or how I feel. Yes, I know how I FEEL - feel for you. But is that because we are HERE, together, whilst Ian is a long way away? Will my feelings for you be the same when Ian returns and demobs? If only you knew how often I wish I had never set eyes on you, never met you or heard of you - only the next minute to bless the day I met you.

Do I feel like this simply because I am loyal to Ian? Is it possible to have feelings like this for two people at the same time? Or do I love you - and only THINK I love Ian?

Oh, Terry - I'm afraid - scared. I don't know what I'm afraid of, but I AM afraid. Scared and happy. Confused. Tell me what I should do!"

Your eyes said more than words. They pleaded - pleaded for what?

That I should love you? That I should, in some magical way, make you forget about Ian?

I wish I could! God knows I wish I could! But all I could do, all I did, was to hold you even tighter, tell you I loved you, over and over again. That I couldn't live without you, that you were part of me. One with me. My world.

Even then, the words sounded like platitudes. Just words. How I wanted to express my feelings, Lulla! How I wanted you to realise, to fully understand my feelings for you! All I could do was to use words---.

Did we notice that the air became cooler as the sun sank

lower and lower? And that we were hungry and thirsty - the trip had turned out longer and quite different from what we had planned?

We did notice that we felt stiff and sore after having sat on the ground for such a long time! How we laughed when we struggled to get up and stretched our arms and legs to let the blood start circulating again! Do you remember? Brushed moss and bits of heather off the windcheaters before we put them on. You were a sight to behold from behind - your windcheater was so crumpled you should think you had slept in it for weeks!

But what did it matter?

We walked - or did we stagger? - along, arms round each other, stopping, kissing, at regular intervals. I was even happier and more in love than I had been only a short time before. Suddenly, you had let me come closer to you, let me be part of your life. I knew you better - and I felt an even stronger desire and need to look after you, protect you, make you happy. Make those eyes smile all the time, and never cry.

You telephoned your mother from the first telephone box we came across - you were afraid she might begin to worry about you - where you were. If something had happened.

But all was well, you said. She hadn't worried - because she knew you were with me.

That's exactly what you told me she said - BECAUSE SHE KNEW YOU WERE WITH ME!

I can still feel that tingling sensation of being elated, proud, delighted. On top of the world.

Just then, I could have walked on water.

Look for new targets.

Higher. See anything? Apart from the road down there, thickly carpeted with bodies? No, it doesn't --. HI - wait a minute! What's that - over there, just in front of the trees? Can't see it clearly from here - only that there's <u>something</u> going on there. Starboard a bit, stick forward - a bit more - down a bit.

Lorries? No --, yes -- three lorries --. But what's the --? It's a plane! A strange place to --, I get it! It's been damaged and had to land, and the lorries are bringing people and equipment to fix it.

That's it!

But what type of plane is it? Never seen that type before. Look at the wings - yes, the wings! It's a YAK. YAK or no YAK - does it matter? It's not one of ours, that's for sure! And WHAT a target! There - they've seen us - they're running towards the vehicles and scrambling on - the first one is moving away. Is a tanker! They were filling fuel! Take that one first - the plane will remain where it is for some time, I should think!

This is the bloody steepest dive I've made a 51 do - ever, with full throttle. But I have to get that tanker before it gets a chance to disappear in between the trees and seek some sort of shelter. It will be more difficult to get it there.

Let go - fire! The distance may be a bit greater than -- but fire ahead of it, a fraction back on the stick. There! The tanker has to turn round a large rock - there: you've got him! In the centre. Wonder if we're taking the tanker all five us, or if someone is taking care of the plane? Perhaps I should have said --.

What the hell! We'll manage --.

The tanker is stopping - it's hit! Some soldiers are jumping off, running - literally - for their life, seeking shelter among the trees. Let them run - take the tanker - the <u>tanker</u>!

Don't go too low!

What did I say? That's what I call an explosion! Fireworks.

Up again -- fast. Are we still five? One, two, -- TWO! Where are the others? Can't see who - YES! There they are. One is busy making small pieces of the aircraft, the other one is covering his back.

Of course: Bill and Sam!

We're still five.

More down there, near us?

There are the 86s. That is, I assume those dots over there are ours - and not MIGs. Not coming from the south. Surely not -?

"Hello, Gimlet Red Leader, Barnet Red Leader calling. Over."

"Hello, Barnet Red Leader, Gimlet Red Leader here. Nice to see you. Over."

"OK, Gimlet - have you any food for us? We are hungry and full of ammunition. Tanks or trains would be welcome.

Over."

"Hello, Barnet. No, nothing particular. We have just shot up a tanker and a YAK on the ground. - Well, if they have YAKs down here, that is. Over."

"They have some, as far as I know. Pushing forward everything they have, I should think. Probably a YAK-9. - Right, we'll take over. Over and out."

The fuel gauge is still showing half full tanks, so we may as well look for --.

"Hello, Gimlet Red Leader and Barnet Red Leader - post SP-370 calling. Over."

"Hello, SP-370, Barnet Red Leader here and taking over for Gimlet - Gimlet stand by. Whats'up? Over."

"SP-370 here. You're looking for fish? We can see you - turn 17° north-northeast until you cross the railway line. Follow it northwards a bit and you'll see a train carrying troops. The 29s have bombed along there, but as far as we know they have repaired the damage and have started sending reinforcements to a point about 2 miles from the river. Our artillery has pulled out and is moving further south, so we can't do much - nothing, in fact. We were ordered to withdraw to new positions to prevent us being overrun.

So what about it - is this something for you? Over."

"Hello, SP-370. You bet it is! Agree, Gimlet? Over."

"Gimlet Red Leader here. Have I ever disagreed with you? Turning to course given. Over and out."

A train. Full of troops. Big fish, that is, Lulla!

⁜⁜⁜

What we did on the Monday after that walk in the mountains, I can't remember. Perhaps I didn't see you. But I remember I rang you. Well, not remember, exactly - but I *know* I did, simply because I rang you every day. Every single day. And several times some days. (You told me once that your boss didn't mind me ringing you at work - he said I sounded so nice, you said!)

But I remember the Tuesday. Of course I do - your mother said you had to invite me home for dinner!

AND I remember what your mother had made for dinner: cauliflower soup, roast beef and pancakes!

It could hardly have been better.

Your mother laughed like a coy schoolgirl when I commented that it was certainly one of the best meals I had had for a very, very long time.

And I meant it, Lulla - I meant it!

And afterwards --. We just sat there and talked. Homely, cosy. Warm and lovely. And you sat next to me. Very close. And your mother made coffee and kept going into the kitchen, leaving us alone.

Happiness. Pure and undiluted happiness.

That's what it was.

Like it should be.

Do you remember the following Saturday? Or perhaps it was the Saturday after that one? It's hard to tell - whenever I was with you, time speeded up to a frantic haste, making it difficult to keep up. How can time - an inanimate object, if object is the right word - possibly change from the rushing speed it always had when we were together, to something near standstill when we were apart?

Don't ask me. I don't know.

Anyway, the Saturday. A friend of mine, or more correctly, a friend of mine and his wife, Charles and Charlotte - immediately christened "Cha-cha" by you, remember? - had a weekend cottage by the sea, near one of the little bays. They invited us out there for the weekend, but we had already bought tickets for the theatre - "The Importance of being Earnest", - if I remember rightly. They didn't think that was a problem — "Just take a taxi out to us straight form the theatre," they said. Which we thought was a good idea.

If only we'd been able to get a taxi that easily! We walked and we walked and did our best to flag down every car that went by, but no taxi. Not for all the tea in China.

Do you remember where we finally ended up? Exactly! At the taxi rank where I had waved goodbye to you that very first evening!

But this time there wasn't only one couple in front of us -

but quite a few. And it took a long time before it was our turn. So long that you said we could not possibly arrive at their cottage this time of night. But I said they were expecting us, and if we did NOT turn up, they would think something was wrong and begin to worry.

So it was well past midnight when we got out of the taxi and walked the four or five minutes down the little track to the cottage.

Or cottages. And that was what made it a bit tricky: I had been there before, but only once, in broad daylight and sunshine, and I hadn't really paid much attention to exactly WHICH cottage was theirs. I seemed to remember it was painted red, with white window frames. As far as we could make out in the darkness, two of the huts were red with white window frames.

It was 50-50.

But both were darker than the night which surrounded us. Whether the occupants expected guests or not, they had quite clearly gone to bed. Or perhaps even worse: gone back home to town.

And what did you do?

There we were, stranded in the middle of the night, locked out from a cottage we didn't know exactly where it was, with the choice of spending a chilly night in the open air or start banging on doors and windows, hoping we would be waking the right people. If indeed they were still there. And not the slightest possibility of any form of transport back to town for many hours. In short: not a happy situation.

But you found it hilarious!

So hilarious that you could hardly talk, merely gasp between the bouts of laughter, point at the cottages, and wipe your tears.

What should we do?

We tossed a mental coin between the two likely cottages, knocked on the door and hoped for the best.

Nothing happened.

We knocked again. On the door and on one of the windows. A light came on - and it wasn't until that moment it struck me that I hadn't the faintest idea what I would say if the door was opened by a total stranger.

It was a great relief to find it was the right one!

And you were right: when it came to midnight, and no sign of us, they had assumed that we had changed our mind and decided to stay in town.

But they did let us in.

Do you think they heard us that night? It wasn't all that easy to be quiet, for all we both did our best. But when I am with you, Lulla, it is not easy to keep a clear head and to think straight. The feelings - warm, strong, and intense feelings - take over and you and I are the only ones in the world.

They were already up when we staggered into the sunlit sitting room - it must have been the smell of coffee.

And I was very, very pleased to see that you and Charlotte got on so well together right from the start. The two of you pushed Charles and I out the door because you wanted to prepare the lunch in peace and quiet – "without any stupid interference," and you both laughed. So Charles and I took the rowing boat and tried our luck at fishing. The fish was far luckier than we were. Bangers and mash - that's what we had. Bangers and mash. With home made ice cream to follow.

"A damned nice girl you've got yourself!" Charlotte said when we cleared the table whilst you were in the kitchen. "Hold on to her!"

Thanks for reminding me, Charlotte!

And then - the NEXT weekend! Do I remember the next weekend! If you don't - ask your mother!

Both of you left on Thursday to visit your aunt - your mother's sister - who lived in a hamlet by the shore of a lake, coming home again Sunday afternoon. I said I would meet you at the bus station and help carry your luggage, an offer which your mother quickly accepted, saying it would be nice to have someone meeting you.

Then, on Sunday morning, you rang me and said that a rock fall had blocked the road completely, and there was no way - literally - you could get home. From what you knew then, it might be Tuesday, or even Wednesday, before they managed to clear the road enough for traffic to get by. And what would your boss say?

What your boss would say was hardly my first concern. My first concern was that I would not see you FOR SEVERAL DAYS! Nearly a whole week without seeing you!

It did not even bear thinking about.

Something had to be done. And quickly. But what? Stranded in a hamlet by a lake, with the only road in - and out! - blocked, how on Earth --?

Where the inspiration - because it *was* an inspiration, Lulla, - came from, I'll never know. But I am pretty certain that had I not been so deeply and intensely in love with you that every minute, every second apart from you was burning agony, consuming any sign of clear thinking and reality, I would never have thought of it.

Never.

But I did: hire a plane and fly in and collect you!

There was a small air-taxi firm in town, do you remember? Started by a chap who had been a bomber pilot during the war. He had a couple of Seabees and got most of his business from flying keen flyfishers up to the many lakes in the mountains, plus some general taxi-flying along the coast, so I rang him and asked what he would charge to fly in to where you were, pick you and your mother up and return. I can't remember the price, but does it matter? Nothing mattered - apart from the fact that we were not together. Every second away from you cost me a life.

One hour later I was on my way.

I didn't know where you were, apart from in the hamlet,

but I felt pretty certain that it was not every day an aeroplane would land on the lake, so the entire population - including visitors - would undoubtedly drop whatever they were doing and dash the quickest way to the lake the moment the plane landed.

Quite frankly, if you and your mother had not come down to the lake, but decided to watch the proceedings from your aunt's windows, I don't know what I would have done. It never crossed my mind. I never had any other plans than to GET there as fast as I could, collect you - and bring you back. If you weren't there--?

I never left it a thought.

But you were!

The first thing that struck me was how the mere eight or ten houses we counted from the air could possibly accommodate what appeared to be a large crowd which quickly gathered as we taxied in to the little wooden pier where a handful of rowing boats were tied up. I was half standing up - as much as the rather tight space permitted - eagerly looking for you. And your face when we came right in and I opened the door and shouted your name! I thought for a moment you would fall in the water!

And your mother!

"Flying!" she said and was very, very excited. "Oh, that will be great - just great! I have never flown before in my life!"

You were obviously the envy of everyone present when you came back, suitcase packed, and climbed onboard. Your mother was much more excited than you were - she was just like a kid on Christmas day, wasn't she? And climbed in next to the pilot without even asking - leaving us to sit behind.

When he started the engine, right behind us, above our heads, (it was a pusher, remember?), you gripped my arm so tight that I thought you would pierce the skin, and when he started taxiing out - you didn't like it, Lulla. Not one little bit! You gripped me even harder, took a deep breath, pressed your head right back and closed your eyes, no doubt wishing you weren't there. And as we gathered speed, finally slipping the water, climbing and turning, - I'll never forget it, and neither will you! Whilst your mother looked and pointed and excitedly asked the pilot what THAT was and what THAT was, your eyes were shut tighter than ever, and your grip really hurt my arm. I am sure you never heard what I said to you, trying to make you relax. RELAX? You were stiff and tense like a wooden doll, Lulla!

You didn't relax much once we were up and levelled out; every time we hit even the slightest turbulence, making the little plane jump and shudder a bit, back came the stiff doll.

I know someone who was mightily, visibly, and audibly relieved when we landed, safe and sound, - you were quicker onto the landing platform than most agile athletes would have managed, Lulla!

Somehow the return trip seemed much, much shorter than the outward trip. Because we were together. See - the same always happened: time sped by when I was with you. I know the clock said about 30 minutes either way, but my brain and body told me the return leg lasted only 5 minutes.

And when we landed --, your mother could hardly believe that it had taken us just about half an hour to get back – and not five hours by bus. I think that's what impressed her most of all.

The next few days might well have been pleasant, if only I could remember them.

But I can't. They disappeared in the terrible explosion the following Thursday.

That's when the world disappeared, blown to smithereens. To dust. To nothing.

Ay least my world. *Our* world.

The moment you stepped off the bus I knew something was wrong. I could feel it. I saw it. But when I asked, you shook your head and said "What do you mean - wrong?" and stuck your arm under mine.

"Can we go to your flat for a little?" you said and smiled.

But your eyes didn't smile, and your dimples were hardly visible.

And no sooner were we inside the door than you threw your arms round me and cried. Sobbed. Your shoulders shaking.

"What on earth IS it, Lulla? What IS it? What's happened?"

I couldn't even imagine what was the matter. What terrible things might have happened.

"Oh, Terry - TERRY!" You were sobbing so hard that it was nearly impossible to understand the few words you managed to get out. "It -- what I have -- you know -- what I have dreaded -- been afraid of -- OH, TERRY!"

I let you cry and sob. Cry and sob. And shake, holding you tight. What else could I do? I had no idea what had happened, and I would have to wait until you had calmed down enough to be able to talk some sense I could understand.

It took a long, long time.

My shoulder was soaking wet from your tears.

"Today," you started, "today - when I came home from the office--."

And stopped.

"Yes, what, Lulla? What happened?"

Suddenly I got a very empty and ice-cold feeling inside me.

"I -- there was -- my mother gave me a telegram which had just arrived."

"Let's sit down," I said and pulled us both onto the settee.

"A telegram," you said again, and stopped.

"It was from Ian," you said, hardly audible, turning your face away. "He's coming home on three weeks' leave. On Saturday. - The day after tomorrow," you added quite unnecessarily.

Did I breathe in? Did I stop breathing? Did I scream?

Shout? Cry? Did I say anything? Nothing? Did I faint?

I have no idea. I cannot remember. I think - THINK - I felt paralysed, paralysed by an ice cold hand gripping the whole of my inside, squeezing tight, twisting and pulling hard. Followed by iron boots, heavy iron boots, kicking me, stamping me down and into the ground.

Hard.

Nor do I know why I should react like that. Surely I should - MUST - have known in my heart of hearts that this day, this terrible, awful day, would come. Sooner or later. The day when you and Ian --.

"Oh, Terry - I am afraid. Afraid that --." You looked at me again.

"Of what?" I heard myself ask. At least it sounded like me. Perhaps it wasn't.

I don't know.

"That you -- I - we. What will happen when I see Ian again - after all we have -- the way I feel for you?"

The world spun round. Crazily. Faster and faster.

IAN! COMING HOME! FOR THREE WEEKS!

"Did you --had you any idea - did you know that he would come home on leave?"

"No, No. Believe me, Terry, I had no idea. He has never said anything, never written a word about it. The intention was -- he said he would not come home until he was demobbed, in many, many months. That is why I -- you know, Terry - oh, God, I have been so scared, so confused -

and yet so happy. So very, very happy! Happy and in love. I love you, Terry - I LOVE you - you must, please! - you must believe me! Not because my mother and others think you are great and like you - that's nothing to do with it. *I* like you - and I am so happy, so utterly happy, when we are together. And that's why I am so frightened, Terry, so terribly scared, that when I meet Ian again -- that --."

You clung to me again and let the tears run freely. Unhindered.

Did I say I would never in my life forget that Thursday?

Not any more than someone who is hit by lightning or blown sideways by an explosion will ever forget it.

True, not all the details as things happened, second by second. Simply all the chaos, the pain, the confusion, the deadly fear. And the long, terribly long, after-effects.

What we talked about - how can you possibly expect me to remember that, now? You had been torn away from me, suddenly, brutally - in a split second the gap between us had become enormous, unbridgeable. I heard you - I spoke to you - but where were you?

"I suppose this is the end, then?" It was me saying that, wasn't it?

"Perhaps we -- you must believe me, Terry - you must believe me when I say that at times - no, OFTEN! - I often think that I -- hope that Ian and I -- that Ian and I -- perhaps have changed so much that we no longer --, that we --."

You looked at me with eyes red from crying. Red, wet and

shiny.

You were beautiful.

"Would you -- will you wait for me, Terry? I mean -- if - if Ian and I don't --, will you -- may I come back to you? That is where I want to be, near you - with you. I am so happy, so relaxed, so FREE when I am with you. It's so EASY being with you, you are so different --."

Did I listen to what you said? Did I realise WHAT you were saying?

"I hoped every day that I would get a letter from Ian," you continued. "A letter saying that it was all over between us - finished. Meaning it was only you and I - us two and nobody else. - Yes of course I thought of writing to *him* - telling him about you -- me - us, but I didn't. I wanted to, Terry, I wanted to, but somehow I never managed to put the words to paper --. And that is what I have been afraid of all this time - afraid that when I saw him again, when we were together again --."

It's a miracle you had any tears left, Lulla!

It is a miracle *I* had any tears left, Lulla!

I held you, tight, as in desperation. It WAS desperation. And you clung to me as were you afraid that *I* would leave *you*! You sobbed, hard and long.

With my tears running as freely as yours.

It was the most horrible, dreadful day of my whole life, with no way out; no hope or light, only utter, total, miserable, and awful darkness. A world without you. Empty. Meaningless.

"I suppose this is the end, then?" At least I think that's what I said.

How could I find sensible words, comforting words, with my world and life in shattered ruins all round me, my brain numbed. If only me feelings had been numbed and paralysed! But they were not, Lulla, they were not! They were running berserk; racing.

"It's best that way," you whispered. "Don't you think it's best that way?"

Did I think so? I don't know what I thought - all I knew was that my Life was Dead. Life the way I had imagined it and hoped it would be - life as I had dreamed about it. It had just started - and now it was over.

How long were we in my flat? Two hours? Three hours? Four or five?

Perhaps we were there a week. I wanted to see you home, but you said no.

"*Please, Terry,*" and you had no more tears, "don't see me home. PLEASE - let me go - just go, now, alone. I'll take a taxi. If you see me home, we'll start all over again, talking --. Please let me go. Now. Alone."

I held you. Very tight. A last time. Hoping it would last an eternity.

We kissed. And cried - more tears from somewhere. They tasted very salty.

"I shall never - NEVER - forget the wonderful time we have had together," you said. "Never ever!"

"Do you think I'll forget it?"

"Will you wait for me if -- if Ian and I --, will you, Terry?"

It was the most inane question I had ever heard. Wait for you!

"I MUST go now, Terry. If I don't leave now -- PLEASE!"

That's what your mouth said. But your eyes, your heart, said something quite different.

You would have made a lousy actress.

The clock struck 3 as I rang for a taxi.

"The driver must think you have been to the party of all parties, the way you look!" I said as I saw you to the taxi, for some totally irrelevant reason trying to sound - sound what? Cheerful? Happy?

Don't be stupid!

But I had to say something to dampen the pain, muffle the shouts for help inside me and the sounds of all my hopes and dreams being so brutally crushed.

Unreal words in an unreal world.

A world where you and I no longer existed.

Don't ask me about the next days. That's when the painful, terrible truth began to sink in. Materialise. Become an unwanted and unwelcome reality. Everything which happened that Thursday evening. If THAT had been terrible, it was as nothing compared to the days which followed.

Nothing.

At first. my brain quite simply refused to believe it all. Or even small parts of it, sending messages to my heart that it was all a terrible misunderstanding - a nightmare from which I would soon wake up. My brain told the rest of me it was nothing but an impossibility that Life could treat or torture anyone in this way.

Impossible.

Hours and days went by in slow motion, and everything merely became worse. And worse. This was no nightmare, no misunderstanding, but a harsh reality.

What I did? Where? When?

I don't know. I really have no idea whatsoever. I have a faint recollection that I just wandered aimlessly about; drugged, paralysed. Can you be paralysed and walk around at the same time?

I think so.

I did.

It was not until the end of the following week I came to, the pain now even worse. But at the same time a hope beyond hope had opened the door ajar to the thought that perhaps you and Ian perhaps --, that you one day would come running towards me, throw yourself into my arms, telling me you couldn't live without me, and that it was just the two of us.

Forever. That WE were meant for each other, made for each other.

Just the two of us in the whole world.

Three weeks, you had said. He would be at home for three weeks.

Isn't it strange how you try, at times even manage, to convince yourself that what you WANT to happen WILL happen? Or perhaps you haven't experienced it.

I have.

As the days dragged by, I told myself that the faint ray of hope that you and Ian might - just MIGHT - have changed so much that -- became brighter and firmer. A seed of hope which had sowed itself.

Or perhaps I had done so.

But it was there - it was there, Lulla!

I saw it! I felt it!

Everything around me reminded me of you. Of us. About the wonderful time we had had together. About life the way it had been, could have been - the only life I could imagine.

Life together with you.

I went to the cinema one evening. And the memories of you - the times we had been to the cinema - flooded in over me like a huge wave, threatening to asphyxiate me. The paralysis returned, the loneliness and helplessness was awful. Terrible.

But where could I go and what could I do without being reminded of you all the time?

You were still everywhere.

Taxis, buses, walks, parks, streets, cinemas - EVERYTHING reminded me of you. Of all we had done. The fun we had had. Places we had been to.

I existed in a vacuum. Can you exist in a vacuum?

It is when the darkness is at its darkest and desperation is at its deepest that hope is at its strongest. Or most desperate.

I hoped. And hoped. An intensely burning hope I did not dare to let go.

Not until it was so brutally and mercilessly crushed. Killed. Obliterated. Pulverised.

I came out from cinema - our favourite cinema - one evening, after having seen - seen what? A film, that's all I know. I just sat there, in the darkness, sat there without taking in what happened on the screen. Thoughts, dreams, and feelings were not disturbed by whatever went on up front.

When the cinema emptied after the film, there was already a long queue for the next performance.

And there, roughly half way along, I spotted you.

My first reaction was an overwhelming desire and need to rush towards you - push everyone in my way aside as if they didn't matter, take you in my arms, kiss you, hold you - tell you I loved you.

Over and over again.

It was not my willpower which kept me back, that's for sure.

You didn't see me. Or if you did, you did not show it. But I think - I HOPE, Lulla, I hope! - you didn't see me.

All you saw was the one next to you. You held one arm round him - you looked up at him and smiled to him in exactly the same way you had looked and smiled at me, a long long time ago. Your eyes were sparkling. Exactly the way they had sparkled when you looked at me.

I had never seen Ian. I didn't know him. But you had mentioned once, a long time ago - LONG TIME AGO? It was only weeks! - that he had blonde, slightly curly hair.

The one next to you had blonde, slightly curly hair.

And you smiled and radiated happiness.

A glowing icicle from space hurtled right through me, tore me apart, and disappeared out the other side of me, taking lumps and shattered bits of me with it back into space.

That is where I died.

There is no need to tell you the rest. Come to think of it, Lulla, I really don't know why I have told you all I have done. Why on earth should you be interested?

No, I am not bitter, Lulla. Not at all. I should not have insisted on seeing you again. And when you told me about Ian; I should have disappeared out of your life, and you out of mine, there and then. It was not fair to you - or to Ian - to carry on, fall in love with you, to let you became part of me, to become my whole life.

I should have kept away.

But I didn't. Couldn't. No way.

It was there, in the cinema queue, you made it clear that I had lost you forever.

That's why I handed in my notice the next day, sold all I had to sell, and disappeared.

And ended up here. In the middle of a war.

How? Does it matter?

Had it not been for that little book --.

***

Big fish even!

There are a lot of us now, but only five 51s. We're all working overtime on killing, maiming, obliterating.

It's war.

"Hello Barnet Red Leader, SP-370 calling again. You are right overhead. Continue on the same course, and you'll see the line."

Right overhead? Good God - are there people DOWN THERE? People in that blackened, burnt, smoking Hell below us? Poor devils!

You notice the difference in speed all right! The 86s are already a long way ahead of us. Seems only a minute since they appeared as dots miles behind us--.

There, they are turning. Due north. Probably the railway line.

Yes, there it is.

Bloody fast, these 86s. Yes, I know I have said it many times before, but where will it all end? How fast will the planes fly in 20 - 30 - 40 years from now? Supersonic? Faster? At what speed will the human body be injured - disintegrate?

When Stephenson built the first railway, many thought that his steam locomotive went so fast that people would become ill, and perhaps die from the forces against the various organs in the body!

Perhaps that's how the human race will exterminate itself: at great speed.

"Hello Gimlet Red Leader, Barnet Red Leader calling.

Over."

"Hello Barnet Red Leader, Gimlet Red Leader here. Over."

"We can see the train. Going in, attacking low. Welcome after us! Over and out!"

They are diving. Steeply.

There's the train. Looks like an armoured train - lots of flak coming up towards the 86s. Slightly over now, get in from the side. But only a little. That's it! Good!

"OK, Gimlet, take one coach at a time. Good luck!"

It is boiling down there. Sand, soil, stones, and pieces of metal are being flung up, only to hang in midair for a second before fluttering down again, disappearing in smoke and dust.

The guns on the train joining in with short, quick tongues of fire.

The steam engine has been hit - it is wrapped in a white shroud of steam. The train's shroud of death.

I'll take that one there, the third one behind the steam engine. That's a gun carriage -let's kill the guns and gunners first; then we can safely concentrate on the rest. All of it. Train and soldiers. The lot.

You should think I would be scared stiff, Lulla! The tracers are streaming up and towards me like coloured strings - gliding silently past in an eerie, unreal manner. Like nice little pearls. But if only one single of them hits me, Lulla, it may be enough.

Only one.

I am afraid, terrified, before we take off, when we sit there, just waiting. And afterwards. That's when the trembling comes.

But in the middle of an attack - in the middle of all the dangers? No. Strange, don't you think?

I think so.

The plane is shaking a little, when I fire. The carriage seems to vibrate rapidly in my gun sight. Stop firing - keep steady - THERE! Let go two rockets.

Tschuiii - I can see the fine stripe of smoke they leave behind.

Up - UP - climb! Fast! More - steeper - more throttle - get up!

Now, level out and take a look. Any hits?

Any hits! WOW! The gun carriage has been torn open like a box of sardines - the whole side has been peeled cleanly off.

They won't fire any more from that one, Lulla!

The train has stopped now. Some of the wagons are burning; two have as good as disappeared, blown to pieces into the landscape, and the soldiers are jumping and running from the wagons still intact.

But they are still firing.

And everything is the usual crazy melée of aircraft, tracers, rockets, smoke, and more aircraft darting in between each other.

The hallmark of our civilasation.

A chaotic world, swirling at a crazy speed.

That's the one they're firing from! Can you see it, Lulla? It looks intact. Strange, how can *anything* survive, let alone be seemingly undamaged, in the burning hell down there?

But it won't be for much longer!

Dive straight at it and soften it up a bit with the machine guns before sending the rockets to seal its fate.

There - to my right - can you see -a plane is falling? Trailing a long tail of smoke and fire behind it.

Smoke and yellow, evil looking flames.

It is a 51, Lulla - it is a 51! Who is it - WHO IS IT? Has he jumped? Who -- who -- where is he!

What ARE you doing? Don't bother about him - don't look at the plane, you idiot! You mustn't - YOU MUSTN'T! Lose your concentration one tenth of a second - one hundredth of a second - and you are finished.

Take the train - THE TRAIN!

It is easier for them to fire now, with the train standing still.

And their aim is bloody good - too bloody good! Look out!

But I'll give them something to think about - two rockets!

But not yet. Further down - further down - to make sure. Absolutely sure. Don't waste any rockets. They have to hit.

Who was shot down, I wonder? Good job Bobby isn't here, but who --?

DON'T THINK ANY MORE ABOUT THAT PLANE! Look at the train. You're further down than you intended; let go the bloody rockets and get up again as fast as you can. NOW!

What's that? It sounds like glass breaking. Strange, I could swear I heard glass breaking. But where?

NOW - let go rockets!

But what is it, Lulla? I can't move my arm! I can't press the button to send the rockets on their way!

This is very odd, - I haven't blackout, because I haven't pulled up yet.

Never had this before --.

Come on, DO get those bloody rockets off!

But where's the train? It has disappeared - it has disappeared, Lulla! In the fog. FOG? Where's the fog come from?

Suddenly - I can't see anything in this fog - where's the bloody fog come from?

And the heat! Better loosen the straps a bit. It's very hot.

My arm - I can't move that arm either, Lulla! What the Hell --?

Lulla - I am hit! I HAVE BEEN HIT!

Can you hear me, Lulla? CAN YOU HEAR ME?

Everything is whirling around - just like the day you told me about the telegram. Then everything went in a spin as well.

Round and round. Spinning.

Strange how silent and pleasant it suddenly is. Quiet, silent - have they stopped firing? Yes, they must have stopped - everything has stopped. Hear - not a sound, Lulla, not a single sound! Silence - only silence. Can -- you -- feel how hot -- I am -- floating -- see, Lulla -- see --- I -- am - floating --.

We must win, Lulla - we -- must -- win. -- For -- the --sake -- of -- the world.

Why --is -- it so-- dark, Lulla -- so dark --. I -- Lulla ---.